THE GROUNDHOG FOREVER

The Groundhog Forever

A NOVEL BY
HENRY HOKE

wtaw press

Published by WTAW Press
PO Box 2825
Santa Rosa, CA 95405
www.wtawpress.org

Edited by Peg Alford Pursell
Cover art by Malcolm Oliver Perkins
Designed by HR Hegnauer

Library of Congress Cataloging-in-Publication Data

Names: Hoke, Henry, author.
Title: The groundhog forever : a novel / Henry Hoke.
Description: Santa Rosa, CA: WTAW Press, 2021.
Identifiers: LCCN: 2020940171 | ISBN 978-1-7329820-5-5 (pbk) |
          978-1-7329820-6-2 (eBook)
Subjects: LCSH Friendship--Fiction. | Gay men--Fiction. | Lesbians--Fiction.
| Gays--Fiction. | September 11 Terrorist Attacks, 2001--Fiction. | New York
(N.Y.)--Fiction. | Murray, Bill, 1950 September 21--Fiction. | Motion pictures--
Production and direction--Fiction. | Alternative histories (Fiction) | Fantasy
fiction. | BISAC FICTION / General | FICTION / LGBT / Gay
Classification: LCC PS3608.O48275 G76 2021 | DDC 813.6--dc23

WTAW Press is a not-for-profit literary press. We are grateful for the assistance
we receive from individual donors.

Thing 2 wanted to die and go to Heaven.

Thing 1 wanted to die and go anywhere but where she was.

Instead they lived and went to New York City.

The object she picked up off the ground turned out to be alive.

"Pass me the bow," he said.

She wiped a grossed-out hand on her pants. "No."

She kept the bow slung over her shoulder. There were no arrows. He followed her to the climbable rock, lugging the camera bag. The climbable rock where they'd planned to shoot their film was surrounded in metal fencing and they couldn't get near it. No signage. For unknown reasons, their location was fucked.

It was a muggy Monday in Central Park. Tuesday would be the last day they would spend on Earth or anywhere else, but at this moment and for the rest of Monday they were pissed, a little at each other but mostly at the hideous city they had sworn not to leave.

So they sat, genuinely defeated on the grass by the fence, holding the bow between them like a tender tug-of-war. They waited for the sky to grant them shadows. They could blend their shadows on the ground and become indistinguishable, one blob, impossible with their actual bodies.

The sun decided to skip their boredom party.

At some point on Wednesday April 28th, everyone who didn't die in the night woke up. Everyone woke up but the two Things. Thing 1 and Thing 2 weren't there on Wednesday to wake up. They had been students as recently as Tuesday, in attendance at the big purple university in Manhattan. But on Wednesday they were nowhere to be found.

Tuesday was their last day.

PART 1
Groundhog Day Day

They woke up on the same day as each other, as usual.

Thing 1 didn't have a roommate, but woke up to the sound of leaving. She had fallen asleep next to someone else. That someone else had just gone to catch a train. Thing 1 dead-bolted the door and got back in bed. She looked at the ceiling and found it wavering, felt she could dive up into it and swim. She closed her eyes until that feeling stopped. She thought about calling Thing 2.

Thing 2 woke up alone in bed, with a roommate across the way. His roommate slept with eyes half-open and let the alarm go off for hours. Thing 2 had to get up and reach over his roommate to mash the clock button and put an end to the beep.

Thing 1 and Thing 2 were probably best friends. They both wanted to make movies and were both in school for that. They became probably best friends fast, when they spent a long bad day together during the first week of freshman classes. When young people spend a long bad day together as strangers, they bond. That long bad day had happened roughly two-and-a-half years of Tuesdays before this Tuesday, which was Groundhog Day Day.

Thing 1 and Thing 2 didn't know it yet, but today, Tuesday, was Groundhog Day Day. They couldn't know. It was April 27th. Months had passed since regular Groundhog Day, and the last ounces of ice from the rodent's foreseen long winter had been shrugged off the trees of Manhattan weeks before.

By most accounts it was an unremarkable morning for the city. A taxi passenger swung their door open without looking and a cyclist crashed through the glass of the window and lay screaming on the shatter of the street. But that happened in SoHo, where Thing 1 and Thing 2 weren't.

Thing 1 and Thing 2 were both in the Middle Village and were brushing their teeth and putting on their clothes and slinging thin spiral notebooks in their backpacks and meeting for lunch and not saying much to each other because after the disappointment of their failed film shoot what was there to say, and walking up to the building where their first class, an afternoon class, was about to happen. These events were muddy in their memory, because they didn't know it was the day that it was. None of these events were the huge event about to happen. They lingered on the sidewalk because there was time and they didn't smoke and they listened to buses mumble.

"Do you see any famous people?"

"No, just their kids."

As they left loud Broadway for the loud lobby and headed down the stairs to class they had no idea who was about to walk through the doors behind them.

The city went so deep that it was hard to feel.

In most places, especially in that part of the island, the city went further down than it did up. By this scale, the basement of school was no lower than a step, a conversation pit.

The subterranean hallway was full of people the Things knew or kind-of-knew. The film program at the university was a large program that felt like a small town. In this small town most people went by nicknames. A professor gave the Things their collective nickname because they had the same swoop of a hairstyle, wore similar clothes, and were always together.

In other ways they were different. She was brown and he was white. People thought of him as a boy and people thought of her as a girl.

"You're a real pair," the professor had declared with her smoke-stained voice.

This naming was a blessing in the world of the film program, the older artist teachers deciding which hungry students to ordain.

Thing 1 and Thing 2 arrived at the open door to class.

Outside the door, the Waterboys were accosting their current professor. Their current professor was an Italian and he'd blessed the Waterboys with their nickname. The Waterboys grew up together in a suburb outside of Chicago where all the famous movies were filmed. They were roommates and co-directors, their ambition and confidence opulent.

"There must be magic in the water where you come from," the Italian had said. "A secret ingredient." So: the Waterboys.

The Waterboys' secret ingredient was, in fact, money, and like anyone with money, they weren't happy with how life was going if they weren't in control. In that moment by the open door of class they were waving a video in the face of the Italian, trying to shift the power position. In his class each Tuesday the Italian would show a different film by someone he considered an auteur, and that auteur would attend class as a guest for questions and answers. The Waterboys considered few of these guests legitimate auteurs. Their favorite auteur was dead and was the subject of the video they were begging the Italian to screen.

"No, no, boys, we are going to watch the movie I have brought." The Italian waved his hand and ducked inside. "It is special. You will see."

The Things barely registered this exchange that first time, because they saw the Waterboys constantly. They were all having a weird dinner together later that night. For homework.

The shorter Waterboy turned to them as they tried to pass. "Are you two okay kissing?" he asked.

Thing 2 looked to Thing 1. Thing 1 responded: "Are you two?"

The Waterboys gazed lovingly into each other's eyes. They moved closer, their lips parting. This wasn't new, wasn't convincing.

The Things went into class. All the rooms in the basement were for film screening. Some cascaded like lecture halls or movie houses. This room was more the intimate, one-level home theater variety. Sixteen students sat in desks facing the Italian and the Things joined them, finding their usual seats in the back right corner. From this vantage point they could judge their classmates without turning around.

The Waterboys moped in last and shut the door behind them.

"Hello." The Italian smirked with mystique and nodded at the projectionist. "We are going to start the movie." The room went dark and the logo of a studio flickered behind him. He sat up front by the Waterboys and the class settled in to watch.

Someone unbelievable was waiting outside.

Cheery music played over clouds and opening credits. The room relaxed. It was the groundhog movie. In contrast to the many inaccessible indulgences of the film program, this movie was from everyone's childhood, a comforting hug. The sinking into seats was audible.

The groundhog movie, released ten years before, tells the story of a middle-aged weatherman who is clearly done with life on its current terms. He is visibly drained by his job and sent to a quaint hamlet to chronicle the arrival of a yearly animal celebrity: the Groundhog Day groundhog. The weatherman's cynical charm repels those around him, and after covering the famous groundhog he finds himself stuck in the quaint hamlet by a blizzard. This is the first level of stuckness in the film.

The second level of stuckness occurs when the weatherman wakes up the next day and it is still Groundhog Day. The same song plays on the alarm clock radio. The same people approach him. It is eerie and it continues to happen.

At first, the weatherman tries all he can to leave the miserable loop. But, once defeated, he uses his temporal advantage to be awful. He steals money, binges calories, and ruins other people's lives. As if, why not.

He convinces himself that his female coworker will be his salvation and that he must pursue her sexually, and configures all his repetitive powers in the service of seducing her. A futile and horrible practice. She perceives his game and remains repulsed. The weatherman decides there's no escaping himself.

A legendary actor named Bill plays the weatherman.

In despair, the weatherman commits suicide, but even this doesn't free him from the same day, the same alarm clock radio song, the same wakeup. It's simply a shortcut. He kills himself again and again, writhes in a snowy purgatory, destroying his body with increasingly inventive flair.

This is a family comedy.

Thing 1 and Thing 2 knew this movie well. They chuckled and nodded and remembered. But halfway through, their attention shifted.

The film program was a society of stragglers. No one else looked back when the door opened a crack and a figure joined the audience. But Thing 2 turned and looked, ever vigilant in collecting fuel for judgment. His mouth opened and he nudged Thing 1, leaning into her ear to whisper:

"It's mother. Fucking. Bill."

Thing 1 turned her head and oh yes, there he was, in a chair by the shadowed door. Bill, aglow in the flickering light of his own image. A shining star from their youth who was now a saint. The Divine Bill. He looked different from the coiffed early nineties brunette man in the groundhog movie. He now had short gray hair and a scraggle of beard. He was glorious.

The Things watched Bill. The Things ceased blinking. Bill watched himself die over and over and over.

The final act of the groundhog movie finds the weatherman coming to an acceptance of his fate, and then righteously attempting to better his circumstances. He leaves his cynicism behind and makes himself skilled, undeniable, generous, a light in the center of everyone's life, radiating and selfless, saving lives. Then all good comes to him, including the affection of his female coworker.

The groundhog movie concludes with the day changing at last. The final scene takes place on the morning of February 3rd. The weatherman will continue into the future, toward death, with the woman of whose love he's made himself worthy.

The movie ended and life started.

Bill stayed in his seat when the lights came up, but by then everyone had seen and everyone stared. Bill wore shorts and an orange Hawaiian-print shirt and a worn yellow visor. He cared so little; they cared so much.

The Italian started a round of applause. Not a standing ovation. Everyone's legs were jelly. Bill rose and stepped forward, took a seat behind a table that the Italian had dragged to the front. He reclined. This space of adulation was his living room.

"So. Let's talk. About the movie, about you, or about me."

No one moved. The Things sat still in the back of the classroom, daring the others to raise their hands. The truly devout don't feel the need to ask questions of the Divine.

"That's a great question," Bill said to the silence. Then the room wasn't quiet anymore.

Laughter and disbelief. Hands hit the air. Bill chose one. Before the student could stammer a question, Bill burst in with "Why am I here? Beats me." And after a pause, "I'm in a new movie with this guy." He gestured to the Italian. "It should be a good one."

Bill signaled for the original asker to go ahead and ask. The asker wondered how many days the weatherman had spent repeating Groundhog Day in the movie.

"I lost count," said Bill, and looked to the Italian. "Okay, your turn." The Italian took over, asked a series of fundamental questions, and for twenty minutes the students paid unprecedented attention. Bill talked about the movie; he talked about himself. Then he queried the class again. "Okay, who's got one?"

The Things watched the taller Waterboy hoist a hand. They could smell the defiance and hoped against hope that he wouldn't be chosen. And he was.

His question, snide, was about an article that had just come out in a major magazine. The article was a profile of the groundhog movie's director, also the director of many other movies starring Bill. It framed this director as the real maestro of a new movement in comedy, the inventor of the dry humorous everyman, an unstoppable cynical emergence. Since this class revolved around auteurs, the Waterboy asked a patient Bill, was there any truth there?

"Well, you can't believe every article you read about yourself," Bill said, and pretended to give the question more thought. "You know, they called me for a comment on that article. They didn't use it, though. I told them I helped bring the guy in to direct that first movie. So, you know. Maybe I invented him."

Thing 2 was raised with religion. His father was a minister. Thing 1 was not raised with religion. Her father was dead.

This class period, in the thrall of Bill, was their first true church.

"Okay, what else do you want from me?" Bill asked, and the class looked around with their minds while their eyes stayed glued on him. "I heard a really good joke the other day, from my brother."

"Can we hear it?" asked the Italian.

"I forgot it." The laughter of disappointment filled the room. "Someone give me their phone, I don't have mine."

As eagerly as their hands had erupted up to question The Divine Bill, now the students hoisted their rainbow of cell phones. A lot of young people had just bought their first cell phones at that point, mostly the flip-open variety. Bill gestured to a pink one, held by a redhead. "I'll have that one." The redhead brought it forward. He dialed a number and waited, the pink resting at his ear below the yellow visor, holding one finger up for effect.

Someone answered. "Hey, it's Billy, is my brother there?" He waited for a response and then covered the receiver and addressed the class: "He's playing golf with a Nobel laureate." He returned to the person on the other end, "Do you remember the joke he told us the other day, about ... right. Okay."

He covered the phone again and projected, "The Democratic nominee for president walks into a bar, and the bartender says, "Why the long face?"'

It was the year 2004. Everyone knew the politician Bill was talking about, and they all got it and laughed. The Democratic nominee for president had a literal long face.

"That's not the joke. Hold on." And then he was back on the phone, "Oh, wait, I remember, nevermind. Talk to you soon." He hung up and spun the pink phone on the table like a top. "I'm going to hold on to this. In case I need it later."

Then Bill told the joke. It was an old joke that hinged on the historical depiction of the Irish as alcoholics. The class was captivated. Bill could have told any joke and slayed them. He could have read a grocery list.

When, minutes later, the Things exited the building, it was clear to them that their lives were now a before and after. Students, some who'd had the encounter and many who hadn't, scattered across the busy Broadway sidewalk.

The Italian and Bill left the main doors and turned north. Bill was now incognito behind sunglasses, but the Things knew, and the Things followed. Bill patted the Italian on the back and they rounded the corner to the left, heading toward Washington Square. Thing 2 hesitated but Thing 1 pulled him along and they continued shadowing. Thing 2 kept almost talking. Thing 1 was quiet and watched Bill's gait, tried to mimic it. They were roughly a block behind when Thing 2 let his voice go.

"Bill is just walking down the street. Like anybody else. Like us. We could kiss him." Thing 2 slapped his cheeks with his hands and held them there.

This interrupted Thing 1's stalker trance and she stopped. The Italian and Bill receded into a thick crowd of springtime students in the park.

Thing 1 sucked her teeth and said, "Stop being so performative."

They shut up and they breathed for a good while. When the while was over, they went on a fake date.

"I like movies where everyone dies, because, you know, it makes it easier that they stop existing once the film ends anyway," Thing 1 said to Thing 2 over their dripping falafel sandwiches. Thing 2 nodded, smiled like this was the most charming thought.

It didn't matter what they said. This could all have been improvised. It wasn't even important that sounds came out of their mouths. Their lips moving occasionally between bites would have been fine.

The Waterboys stood outside the café's window with a camera on a tripod. One hunched over and stared into the lens while the other stood back and rubbed the stubble on his jaw. Inside, the Things had to pretend that the Waterboys weren't there. This wasn't hard.

They had decided, semesters ago, to abandon any pursuit of popular narrative filmmaking. They were artists above all. This acting was a cinch. The Things continued to fabricate their back-and-forth for the lens, pulling smiles from one another and from their starstruck day.

"Think about Bill."

"Now think about Bill."

The Waterboys had made movies where they fucked each other, or where one of them played Hitler. They'd spend two grand on costumes for what amounted to one roll of film. The state of being loaded can breed ennui, but the Waterboys had dodged that bullet and come to New York seeking objective perfection. They monitored the Things inside the café like prey until the right action was captured, and then they pounced, banging on the window to signal "cut."

Inside, the spell broke and the Things were met by thumbs up. They smiled real smiles. There was a fondness between the nicknamed four, a slim thread. The Waterboys had been with them on the long bad day years ago, when they all stood together and watched the skyline collapse.

The Things got up from the table. They could easily gift the Waterboys their next scene, some making out on film, some permanent illusion.

Another interior. A hallway and the door to an apartment, the camera set six feet away. The Waterboys and their cash had moved out of the dorms after freshman year. The Things were intimately familiar with the two bedrooms inside; they crashed here every summer while the Waterboys travelled, Manhattan devotion driving Thing 1 and Thing 2 into the arms of greater privilege.

The Things stood close together for the kissing scene.

They'd kissed once before, or Thing 1 had kissed Thing 2. The kiss had happened at a fake party but it was real. Fake parties, like fake dates, were a common happening for film students. Real kisses were a common happening for freshman. Fake parties could happen at any time of day, if the windows were blacked out and the red plastic cups were filled with water instead of alcohol.

It wasn't easy to have real fun at a fake party.

The fake date was simpler. All the Things needed to do in the hallway now was kiss and open the apartment door and fall inside.

With an "action" from the shorter Waterboy, Thing 1 pressed Thing 2 against the door. "Pretend I'm Bill," she purred. Their mouths met for the second time ever.

They had a combustive quality, mouth-to-mouth in the camera lens, a chemistry. From the moment the Waterboys had met them they scouted how the Things shared the energy and enthusiasm of two people in love. Not with each other, with themselves.

They kissed and Thing 1 fumbled in her pants pocket for the keys to the apartment that wasn't hers. They continued to kiss and the keys dropped from her hand and hit the tile floor with a sharp sound and they continued to kiss and knelt together to pick up the keys and they stood back up and continued to kiss and she lifted the keys to the lock and dropped them again and they knelt again and continued to kiss and the shot got perpetual.

This was one way for people to join, but it wasn't the way that the Things were striving for in real life.

The continuous kiss was maddening the Waterboys. They loved buying film but they didn't love wasting it. Thing 1 felt their evil eyes and pushed away, aiming the key and relieving the lock with a swift click.

"Okay, that'll work," said the taller Waterboy. Whether or not they were satisfied, the shoot was over. Thing 2 patted a goodbye on the Waterboys' shoulders, and Thing 1 tossed the keys at the camera. They stayed close as they retreated.

"You taste like fucking falafel."

"We both do."

There was only one way out of the hallway and they took it.

The school day wasn't over. There were still nighttime colloquiums awaiting the Things' attendance. Students weren't allowed to choose their colloquium, so they were in separate ones. This was good, in a way, because it meant that they could talk shit about different people when they reunited afterwards.

They made it halfway back to school, but then Washington Square Park halted their walk. They couldn't go to different colloquiums, not after the encounter they'd had in class, the Divine visit.

They took a seat on a wooden bench, still warm from the sunlit day coming to a close. The bench was steps away from the spot where they'd last seen Bill. The spot where they'd lost him.

They would never go to a colloquium again.

They bought a six-pack, without any thrill, because they had both just turned twenty-one. The guy at the fateful deli on the corner of the park, who hadn't once checked their IDs, didn't check their IDs then either. Thing 2 paid because it was his turn.

"Whose place?" Thing 1 said and swung the black plastic bag.

"The roommate is 'entertaining' tonight." Thing 2's roommate was hooking up with a residence assistant. "Did New Rochelle leave?"

"Yeah, she left this morning, like before I got up."

"Are you two still—"

"I don't know."

New Rochelle went to school in one of those vague places above the city. The situation was uncertain.

"Sorry," Thing 2 offered.

"It's whatever. So, mine."

They turned north up Fifth Avenue and walked the three blocks to Thing 1's dorm. It was an old building whose insides had been butchered to accommodate multi-person suites. This meant most floors were sliced into strange configurations, and one result of these slices was Thing 1's room, a single in a warped corner.

Once inside, she went straight for the bottle opener and turned on the TV and computer, both positioned on a desk next to the door. She flicked two caps into the trash and hopped onto the bed across the tiny room, holding out a bottle to Thing 2 so he'd join her, their backs to the wall and their legs straight across Thing 1's diamond-patterned duvet. The beer was bitter in a way they liked, and they downed most of it while watching a season finale and eating dry cereal and speaking the obvious by way of decompression.

"That was amazing today."

"Yeah, I totally want Bill for my very own."

"Why didn't we keep following him?"

"I know."

"Why did we let him get away?"

The credits rolled on the TV and Thing 1 turned it off. Both their attentions slid sideways to the arrowless bow tucked in the corner by the bathroom. It was a sobering reminder, this crucial prop from their foiled shoot. The Divine Bill had cleansed them of Monday's failure, but the muck of fresh memory dripped back and they couldn't dodge. Thing 1 dropped into her desk chair, a vintage chair inherited from her passed-away dad, deep and comfortable.

Fuck, they thought. Their film would have been great, but there was only the one rock. It had to be that rock. They had snapped it on a class photo shoot in Central Park. It was a perfect location and they couldn't let it go. Monday was the only day they had the allotment of equipment covered in their tuition. The school was robbing them.

The action of the film came to both of them in a dream on the same night, an affirmation of their connection beyond the cynical superficial.

"I'm going to bed," Thing 1 said and went into the bathroom to dab toner on her face and pee quietly and run a toothbrush back and forth along her teeth. When she finished she saw that Thing 2 had fallen asleep on top of the covers. She removed the beer from his hand and sat back down in front of her computer to craft an away message. She popped on headphones and cued up an album of an Englishman screaming.

Thing 1's away messages were part of her art practice. She spent absurd amounts of time coming up with meaningful, cryptic slivers that would pop up online if anyone tried to chat with her when she wasn't available. Even though most of her friends were texting, she kept using the online messaging program out of retro affinity, mildly retro, like continuing to purchase hard copies of albums in this age of encroaching digital.

She closed her eyes for a minute and listened, and then she typed: *God is a groundhog by which we measure our pain.*

With this posted, she put the computer to sleep and sat back in her chair, glancing at Thing 2 through tired eyelids. She felt lulled away from any discontent by the certainty that there was a lot more future still to come.

Thing 1 drifted off, dreaming for the last time that tomorrow would be another day.

Thing 2 woke up in his own dorm room to what might have been an alarm. But it wasn't, it was his cell phone ringing. He stood up and answered and found Thing 1's voice on the other end.

"Come back," she said. "I just had a funny thought."

"What?"

"You left, weirdo."

"I know, I'm home."

"No. I just heard you leave."

"What?"

"Are you hungover?" Thing 1 asked.

"No, I feel great."

"Well, I feel not great. Why are you doing this? Come back."

"Doing what? I told you I'm home."

There was a long silence while Thing 2 looked around to make sure he was home.

Thing 1 spat. "Okay, whatever, you have class."

"So do you."

"Yeah," she hung up.

He closed his phone and put it down on a chair and the upper part of his body seemed to hover over the lower. Then an alarm went off for real. His roommate was still asleep as if dead, the same. This was most days. This was not a giveaway. He didn't bother hitting snooze for his roommate because he had to go.

He'd been using his roommate's toothpaste because it had whitening. He figured his roommate would never find out, but he tried not to smile around the room because the pearly beautifulness might give him away. Once he was brushed and clothed and on the street to class, he bought a banana from a bodega and trudged away from any creeping strangeness.

Thing 1 opened her eyes to the sound of her door shutting, an eerie softness, as if the leaver was trying not to wake her. She wondered when in the night she'd moved from her chair to the bed, but her head was foggy. This time she didn't get up to lock the door—it was only Thing 2—but she didn't know why he was ducking out, especially with such quiet. Instead she stretched and reached for her phone and called him and was met with aggressive deception, their back-and-forth muddled by her hangover.

He said, "I know, I'm home."

He said, "I feel great."

He said, "So do you."

She felt a tug of anger. The hierarchy of Thing 1 and Thing 2's numbers was internalized, but not without some vigilant enforcement on Thing 1's part. She had to hang up first, and did.

It was later than she wanted it to be. She rushed herself ready. On the way out she woke up her computer and changed her away message to: *But you had stepped away.*

Then she stepped away. She walked down Fifth Avenue and through the park toward her early class in the main building, because she thought it was Wednesday.

Why wouldn't it be Wednesday?

If it had been Wednesday, the Things would have been late for their required math and science courses.

They both entered lecture halls and they both said "What?" Thing 1 out loud because her lecture hall was empty, Thing 2 under his breath because his lecture hall was full of another class, another professor, a wall of doubt. A few students turned to regard Thing 2, but the professor didn't. Thing 1 and Thing 2 both backed out into the hallways of different floors, checked the classroom numbers, and made their way down to the lobby.

The fact that they were the only people who walked into the echoing lobby at that moment was not a coincidence. All classes in the main building were on a strict schedule, the halls either corpse silent or, at every hour-and-forty-five minutes, chaotic deluges. In the current corpse silence they spotted each other and walked to the center of the lobby near the revolving door.

Thing 2 held his hands up in a defensive pose. "I don't remember leaving this morning, I promise."

Thing 1 half heard, because she looked off through the glass doors, looked at the park. The good weather, when Wednesday had called for rain. A clear blue sky and a hail of questions.

In seconds they were plopped at a table inside the fateful deli, having grabbed large coffees for clarity. A 24-hour news channel ran on the TV above their heads. The news was all war.

This was the fateful deli because the Things had bumped into each other inside it on the morning of the long bad day. This same TV was where they had seen the magnitude of the events, beyond the insanity that played out down the island, in plain view outside the deli's doors. The long bad day was the current commander-in-chief's justification for the new war, much like the old war his father—also a president—had started in the same place, back in the Things' first global memories, before the groundhog movie. This new war waged under different pretenses but for the same reasons. An unnecessary remake.

But the Things weren't thinking about any of this horror as they watched the screen. Although the news showed escalation, showed explosions and grim faces behind podiums, the Things had their eyeballs fixed, motionless and watery, on the date in the corner.

It was Tuesday, April 27th. Again.

The quickest way to get to the bottom of a mystery is to check the basement.

Downstairs in the Broadway building, the scene was entirely too familiar. Each screening room hummed with chatter as the Things rounded a bend into a true mind blow, the Italian and the Waterboys in the doorway. Beyond déjà vu.

The shorter Waterboy mistook the Things' dropped jaws for a desire to talk, and asked, for the second time in two identical days, "Are you two okay kissing?"

"We can't. Tonight," Thing 2 managed.

"Because ... it's not ... tonight," Thing 1 added, and they tumbled down the hall away from an eruption of "wait" from the Waterboys, shutting the world out with a slam of the bathroom door. They ended up in the Women's, which was better for privacy.

They looked at their reflections in the wide spotty mirror, watched each other's realizations. Thing 1 felt like throwing up, not from shock, from the rush that mixed with her hangover. She whacked the sink handle and held her mouth under the faucet to take a long gulp. Thing 2 wanted to ask Thing 1 for a hard face slap to wake him up, but chickened out.

"This is happening to you, too? Right?"

"Yes." She let some water fall from her mouth. "Yes."

They hadn't reached overjoyed just yet, but they could see overjoyed in the distance and they were speeding toward it.

They could sense it before it happened. The bathroom door felt vault-heavy with anticipatory weight as they teamworked it open. They'd taken a half hour of calm breaths and were somewhat ready as they crept back to the classroom door. There he was, rubbing the back of his neck and looking off, head cocked to the side to listen in for a movie moment. The Divine Bill, the only other living person in the hallway with the Things, on the planet with the Things.

He looked at the Things without any dose of surprise, full cool, and lifted a beautiful finger vertically across his smirk, a shush. They stepped up near him and nodded to indicate they were due in the class. There was a screech of tires and a sting of music from the movie inside.

"I'm ready, if you guys are." He cracked the door and they went inside as a trio.

The three seats they'd all held on the previous day were vacant. Bill took his and the Things took theirs. The Things kept their heads turned to Bill for the remainder of the screening, full disbelief, not caring if he noticed.

When the lights came on and Bill took his place at the front of the class, the Things sat as silently as they had the first time and watched the exact same events unfold, the same timing, the same questions, the same eruptions of laughter like a track. There was no nervousness, only awe at how their observer status had been upgraded. The mediocrity around them was no longer an itch, as they had transcended it.

While Bill told his final joke to cap off the class, Thing 2 leaned into Thing 1 and whispered, "I've heard this one before," and she used her whole hand to cover his face.

The Things stayed in their seats long after everyone left the class, after the Italian escorted Bill into the hallway with a drove of students tagging along, and after the Waterboys shot them glares while enlisting two other students to star in their precious fake date. They watched as the teaching assistant removed the groundhog movie from the screening console and placed it back in its case. You can't contain it, Thing 1 thought; it's already escaped.

"Could y'all get the lights?" The TA asked over her shoulder as she hustled out. The Things stared at the blank screen and the blank screen stared back. They were hungry and they stood.

"Leave your backpack," commanded Thing 1, dropping her own. "They'll come back to us." They forgot to get the lights.

They sprinted across the street to a pizza place. The Things had grown up with food issues. It was freeing to order slices smothered in baked ziti.

As the carbs filled Thing 2's stomach, so did doubt.

"What if we only get one repeat?" he asked.

"What if," she answered.

"What if it doesn't happen again?"

"What if."

This wasn't a realistic story anymore. For the Things, life was finally making sense.

PART 2
The Vicious Sequel

It happened again.

On that third Tuesday, April 27th, to be sure, they decided to re-create the first Tuesday April 27th: the sleeping in, the quiet lunch, the dutiful attendance of the Divine class, feigning ignorance. Then when the moment presented itself, when Bill asked for questions, they found their bravery and raised their hands.

Thing 1 was called on and spoke for them, like they'd planned.

"What if we told you that what happens to you in the movie is happening to us, now. That this is our third time repeating today, with you, and everyone."

Bill kept his smirk and said, after a pause, "Are you going to tell me that?"

"Yes!" Thing 2 said, too eagerly.

"Both of you?" Bill said. "Lucky."

The eyes of their classmates might as well have been groans. This unfunny bit was now overstaying its welcome. The Things were stone-faced. Bill relieved the pressure. "Well, you don't need to convince me. You've already convinced yourselves, clearly."

Thing 1 got up and left class, unbelieved, and Thing 2 followed. They waited outside across Broadway for Bill to emerge with the Italian, and he did, on schedule. This wasn't the time for a confrontation. They'd have to follow some, and they did, a block behind, as the Italian walked with Bill into the park. The Things joined the crowd that obscured Bill's orange Hawaiian shirt, left with only the bobbing yellow visor as a guiding light. They elbowed past their fellow students to stay in pursuit.

There was a clearing near the dog park and the Italian re-emerged, alone, as if the Divine Bill and his bright colors had evaporated. The Things felt a chill of defeat but it quickly gave way to a new sensation: the heat from a passed torch. Bill was no longer the star of this, they were. They retraced the film shoot that evening, for closure.

They consumed their falafel with genuine pleasure on the fake date. This was their go-to falafel—they ate this falafel multiple times a week—but this time eating it felt like the last time, and was. They played their roles, obedient for the Waterboys. In the hallway they went for a quick kissing scene and door-click, a hello kiss for the camera, a farewell kiss for the Waterboys.

On the fourth repeated Tuesday, and on every one after, they emailed the Waterboys to cancel. They did it first thing, taking turns. The excuses were always unique:

Family tragedy.
Projectile vomiting.
Dead leg.

But the motivation was always the same. There was no room for fake now that a genuine high concept had overtaken their eternity. They had an exclusive contract.

Relieved of obligations, the Things stayed inside all day, silent in their underwear, and instant messaged each other online.

Thing2:   *What time do u wake up?*
Thing1:   *9:40*
Thing2:   *alarm?*
Thing1:   *no, that's when New Rochelle leaves... u?*
Thing2:   *1030, roommate alarm*
Thing1:   *so i can wake u up early but you can never wake me up early*
Thing2:   *I guess*
Thing1:   *typical*
Thing2:   *did u dream?*
Thing1:   *can't remember*
Thing2:   *will we always have the same ones*
Thing1:   *this is the dream.*
Thing2:   *WOAH existential*

Thing 1 minimized the chat window for a minute and put on a loud ballad.

The chat window popped back up.

Thing2:   *How do we know it's only us?*
Thing1:   *woah. Existentialllllll*

Thing 2's roommate got up and prepared for his classes, ignoring Thing 2 entirely up until and including the moment he exited the dorm, like any other day.

Thing2:   *it's only us*

In the privacy of her room, Thing 1 glanced at the clock on the computer screen.

Thing1: *Bill is there right now*
Thing2: *we're missing him*
Thing1: *can't just go see him every day*
Thing2: *too predictable*
Thing1: *i don't want him to get old*
Thing2: *he won't!*
Thing1: *WE won't!*
Thing2: *i'm not gonna lose my hair*
Thing1: *i'm not gonna WASH my hair*

Late that afternoon, Thing 2's roommate returned and began tidying up and throwing passive aggressive weight around.

Thing2: *The RA is about to come over*
Thing1: *come to mine let's get a Dinner*
Thing2: *where*
Thing1: *somewhere... momentous*

Thing 2 stood up and looked in his closet, sat back down and typed *I don't have anything to wear for momentous* and got Thing 1's away message: *In our fantasies we're still insecure.*

They had never been to a momentous restaurant on their own, someplace up high or tucked away. Besides fifty bucks cash from a birthday card, Declining Dollars were all Thing 2 had. Declining Dollars were connected to his purple university ID and could only be used in dining halls and certain neighborhood stores. A monthly amount paid for in advance by his parents and rationed. He'd spent them all at the record store, as usual, on the first of the month. They were mere days away from replenishing. Oh well.

Thing 1 had a credit card with a five hundred dollar limit. "For emergencies only," her mother had warned. What was an emergency, if not this?

"We need the confidence of the immortal," Thing 1 said to Thing 2 as they sat on her bed with a small pile of possible clothes. She was aiming for a restaurant in an atrium nearby where they would normally have to be Divine like Bill to gain access. "We are immortal, hold onto that."

With the confidence of the immortal they dressed up in Thing 1's clothes. With the confidence of the immortal they strode in and were seated. "No plums!" they said to the server, with the confidence of the immortal. They'd both had bad plum experiences as children. Immortals don't fuck with food that repulses them.

It seemed fitting to be bratty in this glass-roofed environment, at least when the server wasn't within earshot. In the movies of their childhood the realization of a magical shift was cause for celebration. They were in Manhattan, not some frozen hamlet. This was only one of an eternity of restaurants.

Thing 2 said, "I wish they wouldn't refill my water every minute, I want to feel like I'm making progress."

Thing 1 said, "I wish everyone could see me the way I see my own reflection in this knife."

Every dish was art, and cuisine is the most temporal art. It got swallowed like Tuesday.

On the fifth 27th they made a mutual decision to lose count. If they let this day get away from them, life could become a montage. As a shortcut, they grabbed a six-pack each at eleven in the morning. If Thing 2 was always going to wake up fine, and Thing 1 was always going to wake up hung over, what was the harm? They drank in the streets and drank in the streets.

People around them seemed to be enjoying the city in the good weather. Enjoying the city in the good weather was for tourists. The Things had to prove against the odds they were real New Yorkers, prove that their surroundings, in some way, belonged to them. They spent the afternoon asking for directions to places they knew damn well how to get to. No matter the answer, they screamed out "wrong" and sprinted away.

This wasn't bad, but still, the days of indulgence might get old, they agreed.

"We'll have to work out a better plan tomorrow."

"Yeah, Wednesday."

Thing 2 held the six-pack with one hand and clutched his sore neck with the other.

"I should have only used one pillow. Two was overkill."

There was a crooked alley a few blocks from school and they wound up there as the light waned. *Hello Sunshine* was written on the ground in chalk. Thing 1 erased the *S*.

They weren't letting the day get away; they had the process backwards. They were getting away from the day.

They couldn't get away from it for long.

Drunkenness pulled the moon down. It was half-full but huge. Thing 1 pointed up as they trudged along Third Avenue. "I like the moon when it's close, like really close, like we're dating, like I need to call it off."

A cab mistook her extended finger for a signal and pulled over beside them. They did what they normally wouldn't and got in. The address was on the tip of both their tongues before Thing 2 gave it a voice, and the cab motored them toward the rock, toward the site of Monday's cinematic failure. Monday seemed like a long time ago, but the disappointment remained fresh, the helplessness.

They must have dozed off as the cross streets flew by because they opened their eyes and were standing on Central Park West. Through the trees they could see klieg lights and white bounces, and they headed in, approached these beacons. A bride and groom stood in the meadow, cheesing for the false illumination.

At the edges of the light was their dream rock, and now it was doubly compromised. Safety netting draped over every inch, additional ugliness beyond the prohibitive fence. Thing 1 leaned against the fence and said, "We'd never be able to screen it for anyone anyway."

In their minds Manhattan Island and the apocalypse were the same thing. The Things were constantly beginning again while the city was constantly ending. The birds that flocked through canyons flanking the park could care less.

When the city turns on its dwellers it doesn't do so lightly.

Thing 1 stood in the bathroom and debated the need to brush her eternal teeth. Thing 2 sat using Thing 1's computer. It felt right to end their days in her dorm room, this cozy abnormal space.

Thing 2 read a short email from his mother, an email that he'd missed on previous iterations. He knew that she was about to go to sleep when she wrote it, about to say her prayers, down south. He knew that if he replied there'd be no way she'd see it until after six the next morning, when he'd already have jumped back. Defiant of time, he typed and sent sonly XOXOs into the void, in hopes that she'd be restless, or rise early and check.

A melancholy slid into his insides with the last of the beer. They decided to sleep, side-by-side on the bed, and for hours they couldn't. Thing 2 waited, awake, to teleport away. Thing 1 waited for him to be gone.

Thing 2 coughed and shifted. "I think I'm getting sick," he said.

"You won't," said Thing 1.

He rolled over and faced the wall.

"It sucks."

"What?" she asked, drowsy.

"I was really kinda looking forward to 2005. Looking forward to having a new president."

Thing 1 and Thing 2 decided they had superpowers. Besides knowing the short future of Tuesday, they could also stay up all night, no sleep necessary, because they'd always be rested at the same level upon waking. All superpowered people need a code. They sat in Thing 1's dorm and made separate lists, word-processed and handwritten. Thing 1 titled hers *The Code: what we won't do.* Thing 2 titled his *Dumb stuff we never have to worry about now that we have forever.*

Never hook up with a soldier, typed Thing 1.

Student loans, wrote Thing 2.

Never leave the city (not even Brooklyn), typed Thing 1.

Having a career, wrote Thing 2.

Their lists grew comically long. They could see the world shrinking, and were gleeful. Each line they wrote felt like a goodbye, like they were waving from a train at a person sprinting down the platform, a person they were ecstatic about not having to see again.

As they wrote they considered the absence of consequence. Thing 2 thought of a TV personality he loathed. Thing 1 fixated on the professor who always squeezed her shoulders in the hallway. Violence inside them swelled and abated. And simultaneously—Thing 2 on his notepad and Thing 1 on her computer—they added: *We do not torture.*

We do not torture.

If they could time travel they'd be able to see themselves from the outside, in the act of list making, and they'd laugh. They must have looked ridiculous, working hard on manifestos that would disappear with the morning, every bit of ink and every digital tally mark gone. But there was only one version of them, locked inside their bodies. They didn't have the privilege and excitement of narrowly avoiding other versions of themselves to prevent paradoxes and catastrophes. That happened in some other movie.

On page five of Thing 2's notebook this futility hit him and he ripped out the pages, balled them up, and threw them into the bathroom, missing the tub by inches. Thing 1 turned and looked at the crumple.

"I'll remember the important ones," Thing 2 promised.

Thing 1 went back to her document and put a finishing touch on the third page, making sure to save the changes. Saving changes felt important if they couldn't effect real change, or couldn't see the effects of that change.

"Can we change the fact that one shitty thing someone says about you can haunt you every day for the rest of your life?" she asked.

"No, but that happens with good things though, too," he countered.

"C'mon, you know that's not true."

Their real superpower was impermanence.

People with superpowers also need missions. Thing 1 went first. "Ask me what I've never done."

"What have you never done?" Thing 2 complied.

"I've never broken up with someone."

She'd been broken up with, though, a handful of times, times she'd largely repressed. The first time she'd been dumped via answering machine at the end of a summer spent apart before middle school started. She could still remember the boy's voice but she couldn't remember his face.

"It has to be in person," she said, and thought of New Rochelle's outstretched hands.

At Thing 2's request, as they sat on the bed in what was now their ritual, Thing 1 recounted the Monday night spent with New Rochelle. "I asked her why she was having trouble sleeping and she said she was thinking of Palestine." They called it Monday night, always, to signify that bygone naturalistic time, in place of last night. Last night was fast becoming a meaningless phrase.

New Rochelle's leaving every morning already bordered on permanent abandonment, and Thing 1 couldn't let this be the final word. "I think I can catch her next time," Thing 1 said and cracked just one knuckle of one finger.

Thing 1 felt the punch of New Rochelle shutting the door, and as usual it pulled her eyes open. She shouted, "Wait," but only a hoarse rasp popped out. She gulped and swung up to perch on the edge of the bed and try another, and this time the "wait" worked but bounced off the closed door and the thick old walls, and she knew it had gone unheard. She swung open the door to see the emptiness that stretched to the curve in the hall, and belted the loudest "hey" she could manage around it.

There was no echo and no response and as she waited for New Rochelle's possible return, she looked down and remembered how little she was wearing. Embarrassment seemed stupid, but she shut the door and went to her drawer for pants and a shirt, anticipating footsteps to signal New Rochelle's return. None came.

She went to the door again, and before opening it, felt woozy from all the dressing and thought better of running out. Instead, she sat down and stirred the possibilities around in her mind, how the confrontation would go:

"I don't know what this is but I don't want to do it anymore, I'm sorry," she might say.

She imagined stoic silence from New Rochelle, then, "Can I have my bow back?" New Rochelle might demand. They'd borrowed the bow for their film shoot from New Rochelle; she made weaponry for a fantastical afterschool program.

"Yes, take it, take it all," Thing 1 imagined she might say, a solid ending blow. This was all projecting. Projecting bloomed a lot from the stuckness.

She sat and felt sick, but she was more than ready to hurt someone's feelings.

When she could manage to stand, Thing 1 called Thing 2 to wake him and share how she'd struck out. They started to work out a plan. Since Thing 1 had the power to wake Thing 2 early, he would hustle over a few avenue blocks and intercept New Rochelle downstairs or on the street or as close as he could make it to her escape path. New Rochelle didn't own a cell phone, couldn't be stopped with a "come back" call.

"What do I say?" he asked. He'd only met New Rochelle once. She mostly steered clear of the film school and any of Thing 1's friends.

"Just tell her I forgot to give her her bow."

"What if she doesn't want it?"

"Figure it out. You feel great and I'm all messed up, so it's your duty."

She scrunched her hand around her hair and envisioned New Rochelle's train chugging north, New Rochelle gazing out the window, indifferent to the space growing between her and the city and the girl in it. Thing 2's voice punctured the thought bubble.

"You want to hang out?"

"No, I want to go back to sleep."

"Me too."

Thing 2 had worn passable basketball shorts and a T-shirt to bed, another advantage. When his cell phone woke him he was able to obediently toss his shoes on and sprint toward Thing 1's dorm without so much as hearing her voice on the other end of the line. To others, he probably looked like a scrawny out-of-shaper doing his first run in a while, but he had a jolt of purpose rocket-fueling him all the way to the claustrophobic lobby of the Fifth Avenue building. New Rochelle wasn't there. He waved to the security guard and found the left stairwell, stood for a moment and listened for anyone coming down, keeping one eye on the square glass panel back into the lobby to see if she emerged from the opposite side, which she didn't.

It was an off-hour, most dorm residents already ensnared in their morning classes or hunkered down sleeping. He saw only a couple people pass, neither with any semblance of the curly mane that he knew New Rochelle to have. Since Thing 1 only lived on the third floor, after ten minutes of waiting, Thing 2 went back into the lobby and stood before the two ancient elevators. The one on the right was broken, its doors blocked by a sign. The one on the left was coming up from the basement. It opened and he saw one person inside, shielded behind a hamper full of clean laundry. He looked back at the guard, made awkward eye contact, and decided to step into the elevator to avoid weirdness. Social conditioning was hard to shake.

"What floor do you want?" said the girl behind the laundry. Thing 2 looked at the button for floor three, already pressed.

"Um, PH," he panicked. "I got it," and he pushed the highest option. At least once they got to floor three he could see if New Rochelle was there, waiting to go down.

"Hey!" said the girl behind the laundry, a familiar face, Thing 2 now noticed, from Cinema Studies.

"Oh, hey," he replied, with an attempted smile.

"Where's Thing 1?" she asked.

"Um—"

"Are you two ... together?"

"No," he replied. "We're in a relationship with today."

The door opened and no one was waiting on floor three. To make sure, Thing 1 leaned out and looked both ways while he held the door open for the bobbing laundry hamper.

"We should hang out sometime," the girl behind the laundry said from the hallway. "I feel like every conversation we've had is about the film program."

"Well, what else is there?" Thing 2 asked, as the door closed.

Thing 2 rode all the way up to PH. It wasn't a legit penthouse, just more dorms. Thing 2 took the stairs down to Thing 1's room to confirm his failure.

The Things didn't catch New Rochelle on the next few tries. Thing 1 lost faith in Thing 2 and stumbled out and into the hallway, but she met him in the stairwell on one repeat, at the elevator on another, their quarry never between them. Thing 2 circled the blocks around the dorm looking, checking delis, imagined turning a corner and bumping into New Rochelle's hair, but it wasn't meant to be.

They couldn't imagine how she was eluding them, how they were fucking this up. They had the numbers, the advantage. There was no bigger advantage than to wake up every morning and find everyone else still the same.

Thing 1 stepped inside her windowless bathroom and closed the door without turning on the light. In the darkness, she wasn't there, in the mirror or anywhere else. The room wasn't there. She was erased in the darkness.

Outside of the darkness, New Rochelle got farther and farther away.

Thing 2 considered New Rochelle a lost cause, but Thing 1 wasn't ready to give up. She had one more longshot in mind: Grand Central. She knew the train New Rochelle left to take, the time and the destination.

But no matter what cab they grabbed or subway they dove into, New Rochelle was already on the train and beyond their reach when they arrived in the atrium of the station. It went without saying that Thing 1 wasn't chasing beyond Manhattan's limits.

"You could always do it by phone, when she gets home," Thing 2 suggested, but then shuddered at the never in Thing 1's glare. "I'm sorry," he said, looking at the big clock above their heads. "I'm not usually up yet." The space was vast and golden and people were moving quickly, upset. The Things stepped outside.

New Rochelle was as unreachable as if she had taken off in a plane, crossing time zones to an island in the Pacific, an angel already. The sun hit them both from behind. They looked at the street and finally realized what they had missed in all previous repetitions, what had been absent the entire time. When the sun hit them, they no longer cast shadows.

If he had the ability to go back to any day, Thing 2 might go back to being a kid, before his major was declared, to his house in the country near the airport. From the first sermon he'd heard his father give, Thing 2 had been obsessed with the afterlife. It went beyond faith to fixation. He spent the weeks and years in between Sundays watching planes from his bedroom window and drawing storyboards of what Heaven might look like. He drew a fuchsia music video, a coastal city.

His mother took him to visit colleges. San Francisco was like a rock at the end of the world. In Los Angeles he could tell that every tour guide was lying to him. It had to be New York, and in New York, he wasn't sure.

Thing 1 was sure. She came from a town outside that rock at the end of the world, a town preserved in the style of an earlier decade, a place where her father felt most American. When she was little he told her he would someday take her to where he'd been born and grew up, somewhere far away across an ocean. But then he died and the idea of his birthplace became sad.

Thing 1 got into palindromes, the reversibility of them. Her name was a palindrome.

The first away message she had ever typed was *Go hang a salami I'm a nostalgia god.*

She wanted to get as far away from her hometown as possible, to the city at the other end of America, and stay away.

As soon as I leave I'm not going anywhere, she thought.

She had chosen her place. If she had to choose a day to repeat, Tuesday was as good as any.

Thing 1 woke up on April 27th and made her away message *There are 8 million stories in the stupid city: you're an idiot*, woke up and made her away message *You wanna go where everybody knows your pain*, woke up and made her away message *Each day is a gift/curse/curse/gift, especially this day.*

Her dead fallen shampooed strands of hair anemonied up from the mesh in the shower drain.

Can you stay under the hot water for an entire day?

The answer is yes.

For two days?

Also, yes.

Three?

"Not if you want to stay friends," Thing 2 said on the other end of the phone when Thing 1 finally sloshed to it. "Come on," said Thing 2. It was his turn for a mission.

Thing 1 looked down at her wrinkled toes. Pruning for hours under the shower scald was a way to simulate old age, but a half-measure. I'm not becoming some other person, she thought. I am her.

Thing 2 sat for days while Thing 1 showered, but he couldn't come up with a calling. He went on the internet and looked up groundhogs. The scientific designation for a group of them was a repetition. Maybe my calling involves animals, he thought, and closed the browser. He had never had an animal, but he related to the fucking groundhog.

After the first day of failed door knocks and unanswered messages from Thing 1, Thing 2 walked south to the university gym to sign up for the equestrian society. This was a hurdle because he'd always been afraid of horses, but each repeated day added distance between him and his childhood fears. The University Equestrians required a deposit, but he had forgotten his checkbook, had forgotten to own a checkbook. This was no problem; he'd acquired a knack for giving up.

He made sure to vacate his dorm each evening so that his roommate could welcome the RA, and he traversed the Middle Village avoiding eye contact with people he knew and trying to find a vantage point to think. On the second night alone, he ended up mutually appreciating a dog with strangers, joining a cluster of young couples to pet the bear-like creature's irresistible fur. As he watched the owner walk the dog down Sullivan Street, he felt a twinge of possibility. He went after the owner and dog as they pawed south, concocting a heist in his last minutes before vanishing. That animal could be his animal.

He followed them to SoHo, the first in a series of mistakes.

"It's a sequel because there are two of us," Thing 2 said, and convinced her. Thing 1 made her way slowly east to meet. Thing 2's dorm was new and had a large open lobby like a hospital. This was her first time setting foot in his building, and she didn't like it. There was no history in this fluorescent mess.

Thing 2 had laid out his mission over the phone. Today they'd keep a constant eye on the apartment of the desired pet, observe the schedule of the owner, the comings and goings and walks that would reveal an absent-minded moment for Thing 2 to swoop in. Thing 1 knew he was aping the groundhog movie with this plot, the way Bill's weatherman lifts a cash satchel from an armored car at the perfect moment, his prescience allowing for the perfect crime. Thing 2 was envisioning a similar fluidity for their capture of this dog, and Thing 1 doubted his confidence.

She stood in the dorm lobby and waited for Thing 2 to come down. A guy in a purple hoodie stood to her left, also anticipating the descent of some dorm resident. She recognized this guy, this near-nobody. One time he'd stood in a crowd of dudes on the sidewalk and shouted "Thank you, come again" at her in the cartoon voice.

Now they shared the liminal. Thing 1 turned to him and said, "That person you're waiting here for? Well I'm waiting here to kill them."

As if, why not.

There was only one passable choice of outfit for Thing 2's Tuesdays: the fitted T-shirt and pants that were clean, folded in the drawer and not balled up in the hamper on that morning and morning and morning. A uniform forever. He transferred the fifty bucks from the birthday card to his wallet, a reminder of his agelessness, and walked to the elevator.

For his birthday, which had just happened a week—now many weeks of Tuesdays—ago, his mother had been in town and taken him out for a dinner at the same place where his father had also spent his twenty-first. A place near Central Park that was named that number, the age.

His father couldn't get away to come up, but he was there in the spirit of so many stories about that ridiculous, drunken night he'd spent in this restaurant, stories Thing 2 and his mother could recite.

At a lull in the meal, Thing 2 had lost himself in the eyes of a young guy server and watched too long as he walked back toward the bar. His mother noticed and asked, "Honey, are you a guy guy or a girl guy?" Thing 2 hid an odd smile behind a gulp of wine and didn't answer, or if he did, it didn't satisfy his mother.

"You can be honest with me," she said. "I learned to spot a lie from your father." In a future they wouldn't experience, Thing 2's dad would admit that he'd spent his twenty-first birthday at a dive bar in the south. It had been the following year's birthday, his twenty-second, that he milestoned in New York.

Together, the Things cut a straight line down from Washington Square, passing the library and the campus tour office. On this strip they mostly looked down, not up, to avoid the clear line of sight all the way to the bottom of the island. Some paces ahead a small university tour group was assembled, the leader gesturing southward, parents hanging their heads.

The Things' eyes met and whispered a "yeah."

"It's like taking a stroll down memory lane," he said so the tour could hear.

"Bad memory lane," she added.

For the next block Thing 2 advised vigilance: they might glimpse the dog in mid-walk. Thing 1 still couldn't picture a dog majestic enough to invite abduction, but knew it wasn't the teacup emerging from the pasta shop. "Bear-like," Thing 2 had said.

The complication happened at the next intersection. A taxi passenger swung their door open without looking and a cyclist crashed through the glass of the taxi window and lay screaming in the shatter of the street. His bike was upended and the taxi passenger tried to right it first, thought better of it, and stepped back to the curb to shout apologies while the cyclist continued to howl. The cab driver had his head in his hands on the dash.

Some traffic stopped and some traffic honked. The Things stepped into the intersection, their sneakers crunching shards. Thing 2 forgot about the dog and looked into the slit face of this miserable guy, wearing a helmet but clearly hurt bad, his pale cheekbones a reminder of a certain server. Thing 2 saw a glittering opportunity to be a hero to the cyclist of tomorrow.

The next day they took an alternate street into SoHo, but the lights were against them and they arrived moments after the crash had occurred. It seemed even worse the second time, more unnecessary. Their awareness of the collision was no match for the city's blood thirst.

They stayed on the sidewalk and waited for the ambulance the cab driver called, watched the cyclist carefully lifted to a stretcher and loaded up. There was a gash in his left arm that had been hidden by his position, and it made Thing 2 look away. The passenger of the taxi was on her phone, muttering to a probable boss, unsure what to do. The cops hadn't arrived. The Things left the scene, queasy.

How did he handle peoples' pain, they wondered, the weatherman in the groundhog movie? How did he bear it? How did he ever progress?

Manhattan was proving a sadistic obstacle course. Any street they picked to run down seemed to place them at the intersection seconds too late. This type of extremity seemed unchangeable, a conflict they couldn't reverse.

It took them five tries before Thing 2 jumped in a passing cab instead. "Divide and conquer," he shouted, a finger pointed south for Thing 1 to follow. She watched his cab peel away and took the first good deep breath she'd been able to take in days. She didn't run, trusting the coming destruction, regardless of her pace.

Thing 2 found himself in a Jesus cab. The Jesus cab is ordained to make all green lights. Exhilaration hit as they swung right onto the block before the future crash site. Thing 2 could feel the earliness, the beating of fate to the punch. One car in front of him was the cab. He recognized the back of the passenger's hair. He could jump out and intercept it before it sped forward with the changing light.

He opened his door and the whole cab shuddered. The cyclist smashed through the window next to him, the handlebars of the bike banging up against Thing 2's hip. The cabbie hurled a curse at his windshield, and Thing 2 leapt out of the other door and sprinted to the cyclist, who was crawling feebly up onto the sidewalk. The cyclist rolled over, howling the now-familiar howl, trying to find words as Thing 2 stood over him murmuring sorrys. The hands of the cyclist found their way up and clasped onto Thing 2's shirt, staining it red. There was no way around it. This was a mess that couldn't be cleaned. The broken glass would always find this young man's face.

Thing 2 wrenched his shirt free and stepped backward to the corner, this small tragedy forcing him to look downtown and skyward to what still seemed like a gaping hole. An overwhelming ache.

Hell isn't other people. It's an alarm that no one turns off.

On the next repeated morning Thing 2 left his roommate's clock beeping and made his away message *I'm not with God I'm in Manhattan.* Once they were in person, Thing 1 noticed him trailing off, spacing out, starting half his sentences with "I don't know."

The day before, when Thing 1 had finally made it to the intersection and found Thing 2 despondent in his bloodstained shirt, she suggested they retreat to her dorm and hide out until morning. He spent the evening growing determined in front of the same episodes, wearing one of her oversized sweatshirts. He'd decided what he wanted to do the next day, but he wasn't telling Thing 1.

"I just want to be up high somewhere," was all he had hinted on the phone before they met in the deli. Thing 1 got a coffee, but Thing 2 seemed to need it more. The mind ruled the body and his head was still full of broken glass. She offered a sip but he declined, and she followed as he trudged toward Broadway, toward their film building. It was early for class, but Thing 2 had no intention of going to the basement.

Thing 2 pressed the button on the wall inside and they waited. Thing 1 guessed roof access was what he was after, and she was correct. The elevator arrived at the exact moment they decided to take the stairs.

The Things stepped out onto the top floor and hurried past some offices and down the long corridor that held the TV studios. The stairwell to the roof was at the end, and they could see its foreboding red sign. A studio door opened and one of their acquaintances exited in full Gestapo costume. He beelined to the water fountain but stopped when he saw the Things' gawk. "Don't ask," he said and bent down to hydrate, unabashed in his evil duds.

The door to the roof advertised an alarm, but the Things had been tipped at some point that it was never armed in the daytime. Since it was Tuesday they certainly didn't shiver at the risk. No sound happened. Thing 1 blocked the door open with a brick, in case. Thing 2 had already made his way to the edge.

The roof was above twelve stories, right where superstitious neighboring buildings would be skipping a thirteenth floor. Thing 2 sat down on the ledge, the drop-off to Broadway, and Thing 1 joined him, cautious.

"Bill's in there right about now," Thing 2 began.

"Yeah. It's crazy on any given day we could just choose to see Bill."

"I know."

"What if like the first Bill, on the first Tuesday, was the only real Bill we experienced," Thing 1 continued, "Honestly. And after that, all the Bills were fabricated, made up by our repeating."

"Do you think it's all happening the same down there, same jokes?"

"Probably, I mean, what did we do?"

"Right. Like do we honestly think that our absence is going to make a difference?"

"I miss the rain." Thing 2 looked as sad as he had all day, but it was then that Thing 1 noticed.

"I want to see how much of the movie this really is," he said.

"What?"

"My dad says he's sure everybody accepts the Lord into their hearts right at the moment before death."

Thing 1, through her daily hangover hum, was still not up to speed. She kept conversing.

"My dad used to say he thought we'd all wake up in the ocean," she said.

"Maybe I'll be a jellyfish," Thing 2 replied. "There he is."

Thing 1 followed his gaze down to the street, where Bill, wearing his unmistakable visor, emerged.

"You have to tell me what happens. After. And I'll tell you."

There's a feeling that consumes us, especially when we're young, before the obligation, before the appointment, the leisurely stretch that lets us sit back and relax because we have all the time in the world. Then when the approaching moment arrives, we realize we've misjudged: time is slipping away quickly. We have no time at all. This second part of the feeling slammed into Thing 1 on the roof in that moment, a meteoric revelation as she watched Thing 2's forward lean. She tried inner peace as an escape hatch from what was about to happen.

Breathe in and appreciate the wind on your face. But. Don't flatter the breeze.

He pushed himself off the roof and she pushed herself backward to safety. She closed her eyes and gripped the gravel that blanketed the roof's surface. She hated her sight.

If she had looked over the ledge she would have seen.

Thing 2 didn't hit Bill, but he got close.

Every unlucky witness would talk about it for the rest of their lives, or the remaining hours before dawn.

PART 3
Inciting Incident

What is plain
Goldfish flavor

was the away
message

she posted the day
he died

The long bad day—roughly two-and-a-half years of Tuesdays before the one that wouldn't end—happened at the start of their second week of freshman classes, when the Things were newly arrived to New York City and not yet branded with nicknames.

Anna woke up in her sixth-floor dorm room on Broadway and crawled out of bed to sit at her desk by the window and finish watching a movie on her laptop before she had to get ready for class. Her roommate mirrored this on the other side of the room, sitting dazed at a laptop, the morning light coming from the blue sky at an angle.

As her movie ended, Anna turned to look out the window and what she saw alarmed her.

"Cool," she said.

"What?" her roommate asked, now looking too.

"There was just this plane that flew between the buildings across the street, right across my line of vision."

Anna went quickly to the bathroom and grabbed her toothbrush; class was closing in and her roommate had left. She hurried, blasting an eighties pop song her father liked on the stereo, drowning out any street noise for the ten minutes it took to get presentable and leave.

She took an empty elevator downstairs and walked through the bustling lobby, blinders of haste on, ignoring the others, and left the dorm, turning right onto Tenth Street. There was a rift in the order of the entire island at the exact moment she stepped out. Walking the length of the block, she noticed other pedestrians, a woman weeping, a man holding onto her.

There must have been a suicide, Anna thought as she approached University Place. Someone must have leapt to their death. Her eyes were pointed downward as she rounded the corner and faced south. She was ready for this. She'd seen the chaos of Manhattan on previous visits, people honking and colliding. If she was going to be a real New Yorker, she had to steel herself and stare.

There were people standing in clusters in the street but no body. Everyone was looking up.

It seemed like two bombs had gone off, up there in the towers that overwhelmed the distance at the bottom of the island. Bombs, like the ones that were set off at the base of the buildings when she was little, a passing story in the news. These smoking gapes were much more horrific, but the contrast of the cloudless day transformed the whole image into a movie scene.

Anna walked the remaining blocks to the corner of the park, to the deli where she always picked up her water and energy bars. A mundane routine. When life is a movie already, it seems fine to do the everyday.

She bought her bottle and bar from the young clerk who continued to stare with the rest of the patrons at the TV screen. The image on screen matched the image downtown, the ash. The anchorman was saying "planes."

She backed away from the counter and bumped into a guy whose name she didn't know, but whose face was familiar, and that was enough.

"Two planes."

"Two. So it's not an ... accident."

"No."

"What's your name, again ... sorry."

"Sam," said the future Thing 2.

They had encountered each other before, in a quick moment when they had been mutually introduced by one faculty member to another at a grad student mixer they'd snuck into separately.

"I don't care how you got in, or how you got drinks, I'm just glad you're here," said the jovial faculty member who'd interviewed them both for admittance into the film program. He had them shake hands with a squat, prestigious old professor. "Meet the future," he said to the elderly man.

"I've already seen the past," croaked the elderly man. "Nice to meet you. Where's the bathroom?"

The deli on the long bad day was now fateful, for this, their second encounter.

"I'm Anna."

"Yeah."

They went outside and walked together to class, still magnetized by normalcy despite the increasing bizarreness of the streets in between.

"My mom has gotta be freaking out," Anna said, as they crossed Broadway.

"Oh yeah, mine too," said Sam. "She probably wants to come and take me away right now."

"I hope she wasn't on the second plane."

In the following moment of desperate, sinful laughter, they truly met.

Their literature class in an annex building on Lafayette Street was unceremoniously cancelled once the teacher arrived.

"As most of you have heard, there's been an attack," she said and told them to go back to their homes and get in touch with their loved ones.

"Fuck that," said someone tall, putting his arm around Sam's shoulder as everyone crowded the door to exit. Anna turned to see the two who would one day be the Waterboys. Sam nodded. He knew them from orientation. They didn't introduce themselves to Anna.

"Anna," she said anyway and nodded her head at them both. Her name was already starting to sound out of whack. They nodded back and led the way out.

Sam and Anna followed the boys back to their dorm on Washington Square, talking fast, near-nonsensical in their speculation. There was too much to process as they pushed through groups of people making their way uptown. From each intersection on the south side of the park they caught glimpses downtown, at the smoke billowing higher, obscuring the wounds in the towers. When they arrived at the boys' room, it was a web of technology. Sam tried the landline phone and found it dead while the boys grabbed fancy still cameras and hoisted the straps around their necks, held them at the ready like weapons and trooped back out and into the stairwell with Anna and Sam close behind.

"Let's see how far down we can go."

Their hurried foursome only made it down one flight of stairs before they sensed a change rocking the whole dorm, a collective catching of breath. They took the door into the nearest hallway, heard screams erupting, and ran to the next open door. Inside, on TV, one of the towers collapsed. Dreadful plumes of gray. Their collective stomachs dropped as debris rained down the whole screen of the broadcast.

The guy sitting cross-legged on the floor of the room turned to them, crying, and opened his mouth to speak. Before a sound came out, the four of them were back in the stairwell, taking two stairs at a time, all the way to the ground floor and back out into the square. The Middle Village felt like a safe distance. Most people stood around, defeated and hazy. A crowd had formed at the corner of LaGuardia Place and Washington Square South, next to a construction site. The university was erecting a hideous new student center but only its skeleton existed then. On one of the large girders a lone construction worker perched, holding his hard hat and looking at the lone tower.

The taller boy raised his fancy camera and took a photo of the construction worker. He raised it again and captured the back of Anna's head, parallel and at equal height with the remaining tower. He turned and took a picture of a cop's tears. There were other students and janitorial staff and commuting businesspeople and camera crews all packed together alongside Sam and Anna and the two boys, and they waited with long gasps for the inevitable.

A New York minute can last a long time.

After the second tower collapsed, causing the construction worker to drop into a sitting position on his girder and hang his head, the foursome found themselves sitting around in the boys' dorm, letting the TV tell them what else was going on and booting up their desktop computers. None of them owned cell phones yet, but if they had it wouldn't have mattered: all cell service was down.

Anna logged into her instant messenger and an infestation of alerts popped up, people she knew and kind of knew from high school asking if she was okay, an outpouring of love from all over the country. She quickly fired off responses, told someone to tell her mother, and let Sam log in and do the same in response to his slightly fewer messages.

The boys didn't care about connecting and were glued to the TV instead, watching the ongoing menace. There had been other crashes.

"This is fucking crazy." The shorter one said the obvious, to everyone's appreciation.

There were still planes in the air. Hours stretched and seemed like hours.

Anna left the room and walked to a window at the north end of the hall, watched the Empire State Building and swore to herself that she wasn't retreating. She'd stay in this city until the bitter end, no matter how bad the air quality got, or how much oversaturated blood they donated, or how many blocks the National Guard shut down, no matter how many American flags sprung up like blood weeds, and no matter how many people looked side-eyed at her skin color. Anna's resolve to stay would be cement against every gross askance.

When Sam appeared next to her at the window, she let him join her pact.

From that day on, Tuesday was the day of the week that meant the most to them, before and after they were dubbed Things. Weeks and years accelerated, past professors who wanted them to create art only inspired by the tragic events and the switching of classes and mentors, fast-forwarding like the way a friend fast-forwarded past the moment of silence during the Oscars on their digital video recorder. "We have to make up time."

When they recalled the long bad day, they were both heartbroken and exhilarated, remembering the feeling that the world beyond their stupid milieu was vast, that there were bigger things going on. This worldview put into perspective how little all their bullshit mattered, made them more aware than ever that life was a violent, breathing, vivid thing.

But perspective is nowhere near as important as people think, and at the end of roughly two-and-a-half years and a gaggle of repeated April 27ths, Thing 2 went to the top of the school and dropped to his death in search of an afterlife. In Thing 1's eyes, he broke their pact.

There was no Heaven for Thing 2, or if there was, it was the same as Groundhog Day Day. In the groundhog movie, the weatherman's suicide ends in a cutaway. He wakes up immediately, unharmed. The same happened for Thing 2. He silenced his roommate's alarm with a fluid joy and opened up his laptop to message Thing 1: *hello i'm alive.* Her away message popped up in response: *To make God laugh, tell her you're a man.*

He called instead, and on the second try, after a lot of rings, she answered, hoarse. "Yeah?"

"I just woke up in fucking bed."

"Okay?"

"I'm alive."

"...good?"

"I don't feel any different, or maybe a little."

"Yeah, I don't feel great."

"I know."

"You ... know."

"I don't think I felt any pain, or I maybe blocked it out."

"Hey, can you stop fucking with me, let's just get lunch."

"Let's get sushi. Uptown."

"Okay, no, just meet me in the normal spot. We have class."

"You want to see Bill?"

"What the fuck are you talking about?"

Thing 1 hung up and left Thing 2's mind on a cracking ice floe.

To get even with God
simply wake up
and smell the salicylic acid

The Things sat in a university café and had a uniquely surreal lunch in a lineage of surreal lunches. Thing 1 was quiet and nibbled the same sandwich she'd ordered on the first Tuesday. Thing 2 couldn't eat and also couldn't stop staring at Thing 1's backpack.

"Why are you staring at my backpack," she broke the lull.

"Why do you ... have a backpack?"

"I always ... do."

Thing 1 shook this off and finished her coffee.

"What happened after?" Thing 2 asked.

"After ..."

"Yesterday."

"I don't know. New Rochelle came over with some whiskey. I don't really want to talk about it."

"Yesterday."

"Yeah, asshole, you returned the equipment, right?"

"I ..."

"Right?"

"Yeah, I returned it."

There was a rushing in Thing 2's ears that muffled his hearing. It was like they were standing on opposite sides of a waterfall. He used his other senses instead, trying to feel out what had gone wrong. Thing 1 had the putrid scent of Monday on her.

To make God last
hand her a groundhog

give her feeding instructions
pray

that she follows them

Thing 2 was rudderless and went through the motions, following Thing 1 as she tossed her lunch and walked to the film building on Broadway, nonchalant. He kept almost speaking, but it was difficult to pick the first word.

"Hey," he started.

"Uh-huh?" she said, opening the door for him.

"What day was yesterday, for you?"

She smirked, half inconvenienced and half curious.

"Um ... Monday. Today's Tuesday." She softly patted his face with her palm, three pats, a gentle call to snap out of it. "We have our last Italian."

And then she walked away.

By the time Thing 2 snapped out of it, Thing 1 was already descending the stairs to the basement. He felt as if a killer was waiting for him down there in the darkness of some screening room. He clutched his shoulders where the straps of a backpack would have been, and went anyway.

To make God mad
tell her she's grounded

send her straight
to her room
without any shadow

Thing 1 was down the hallway at the classroom door, encountering the Italian and the Waterboys, miles away from Thing 2. He loped to them. The Waterboys patted his back as he pushed past and joined Thing 1 in their normal seats. He didn't know if he was angry or jealous that she appeared to have a slate wiped clean.

"You didn't cancel with them?" Thing 2 nodded to the Waterboys.

"No, why would we cancel?"

"It was your turn."

"Shhh."

And it all occurred, again, the same as every Tuesday, the groundhog movie filling the room with its warmth, except Thing 2 was utterly alone. When the Divine Bill stepped in, Thing 2 didn't even bother to look. But Thing 1 did, and she leaned into Thing 2's ear and whispered, "Bill. Is. Here."

Thing 2 looked, mechanically, but couldn't feign surprise.

To send God
into a panic

find a hummingbird
at rest

Halfway through all the crushing sameness—the same charm from Bill, the same questions from the Italian—Thing 2 noticed he'd lost his sense of humor. None of this was funny. Thing 1 was eating it up, in her subtle way, he could tell. The chasm between them was growing and he wanted to reach her but had to hold his hands out straight and look at the backs of them to make sure they were solid.

When the Divine Bill opened up to the room for questions with that now-familiar, "Okay, who's got one?" Thing 2 cringed at what was coming. The Waterboy raised his hand, ready to pounce with his long wind, but then Thing 2 noticed a shift, right in his periphery. Thing 1 also raised her hand.

Bill's attention shifted to her. Thing 2 felt caught in a spotlight, shining blindingly down from the cosmos.

"Hit me," said Bill.

Thing 1 asked her question. "So in the movie, when you fake kill yourself, does all that suicide help cure your depression?"

"Good, a light one," Bill stalled to guffaws.

Thing 1 didn't change her expression, waited patiently for an answer. Thing 2 thought maybe his open mouth would never close again.

Bill granted an answer, "Ask the stunt guy."

Thing 1 stood up amongst the laughter that rippled the air, unsatisfied, and this sent a low-level rumble through her peers. She hoisted up her backpack and shoved it into Thing 2's chest, knocking the wind out of him. Then she left the room.

Thing 2 clutched the backpack tight, as if loosening his grip even an inch would make it detonate.

To see God's shallow
stay in the ground

make the ground your own
hog it

Bill said, "Alright," unflapped by Thing 1's exit, and solicited more questions. There were slight variations in the wake. The taller Waterboy was never called on. Bill's answer to the smarmy question hung only in Thing 2's memory or imagination. The two concepts were hard to differentiate at this point. The room was more muted than it had been on the other days, the repetitions and the original.

While the Italian and Bill and the other students filed out, Thing 2 noticed the Waterboys talking to their runners-up, their alternate cast. The cancellation had happened. Thing 2 unzipped Thing 1's backpack. Inside, instead of notebooks, was a chunk of cinderblock. She was fucking with him. He thanked the cinderblock for the pain it caused him, for the loneliness it shattered. He smiled and slung her backpack over one shoulder.

In search of service, he opened his phone and stepped into the hall, walked down and ducked into an empty room near the stairs back to street level. He called Thing 1 at home and on her cell. No answers.

He turned and saw a message written on the dry-erase board: *Want to live a long and fruitful life? Call (212) 998-6881*

He dialed the number and someone immediately picked up. It was a recruiting office for university telemarketing and alumni outreach. They asked if he was interested in making some extra money while in school, flexible hours. Thing 2 said, "Absolutely," and scheduled a job interview for the next day.

God steps out and sees
her shadow
and it is huge
because she is huge

and that's night

she goes back in her hole
and that's day

we're not getting anywhere
with this model

Thing 2 thought maybe Thing 1 would be waiting outside for him, on the spot where he had landed. It seemed like her particular sadistic approach. But where he'd hoped to see Thing 1 he saw only pavement, in no way spotless but not the way he'd left it, when he'd left the world for a split second between Tuesdays.

He decided to drop the backpack. The chunk of cinderblock inside shifted enough to tug his light frame down, and he tripped and landed on his elbow, scraping it raw. He stood, dusting off his pants and watching no one notice.

What's bleeding becomes your most prominent feature.

If Thing 1 had been trying to hurt him, it worked twice.

He walked in a different direction than he had on any other Tuesday, leaving a trail of blood for her to follow.

On the day
that God steps out
of her hole
and sees only earth

she'll lie down
and become the city

bright at all times

Thing 1 walked west, away from the blood of today and the today before. She felt that lying like she had to to Thing 2 was a little like losing her mind, but it's hard to lose your mind when the future doesn't exist. The need to be by the river overtook her steps. She walked slow, in thought, hurrying only to evade catcalls in the blocks between her and the waterfront she craved.

When she last went to bed her wrist was sore from writing, churning out a stack of handwritten poems about groundhogs and God. The dull pain and the poems had disappeared with the morning. The next day hadn't come, like always, but for the first time Tuesday felt different. She'd decided to make this repeat interesting, with deception and a cinderblock as punishment for Thing 2. The look of loss on his stupid face had been less than satisfying, but whatever. Regret felt pointless.

The riverside was quiet when she reached the grass by its edge. As she looked toward New Jersey, she worried it was mortality that made people wise.

Thing 1 sat for hours. She only truly came alive at the end of each repeated day, when her hangover subsided, her brain unmuddied, and certain sensations returned. The sun disappeared over the river and every pier light hit her heart. She almost forgot what day it was. Then someone walked up behind her and covered her eyes with large inescapable hands.

In God city
the park is not your friend

because you've stared
at the pond too long

and confused swans
with mirrors

In a monastic bar where patrons would be chastised for conversing over a whisper, Thing 2 sat, using his hands to lift pints to his lips. Each time the door swung open he turned to look. The thick fries in front of him went uneaten. He stuck a napkin to his drying wound and saw staccato days in the emptying glasses, visions of an unforgiving future alone; all the days they wouldn't get to have.

One day he might have gotten lost. One day he might have visited the nurse.

One day he might have ducked into an auditorium, near-empty, at the new student center, and seen a dark-haired student wailing at the piano. In the unforgivable future this student would become famous, a pop icon. Everyone would, and not for fifteen minutes like the artist had predicted: they'd all become famous for eternity. In the unforgivable future, timeless fame would come to everyone. In the solitary present, it's a window we walk toward but know we won't reach.

He requested the check from the bartender, far too loudly in his tipsiness, and was shushed. His voice was clear and strong. What a great telemarketer he would have made.

Tell the people close to you that you love them
all the time

because you never know
when they might be on the wrong side of a taxi accident
or when they might jump
or when they might wake up on the day before
every day
for eternity in some kind of
long
cinematic
joke

whatever

people are fleeting

tell them you love them
now today this minute
every minute

shellac yourself to them and roar I love you over and over until you
lose your voice

watch everyone else do this
until life is just open mouths and moony eyes
inches away in a writhe

do that and regret will get vanquished

do that and win

Thing 2 spent the remnants of his birthday money on a cab to Thing 1's dorm. The cab driver asked what Thing 2 did, and he said he was a film student. The cab driver asked him what he was working on. He was hesitant, but he was also drunk. He let fly.

"My dream is to make a TV show and my TV show is called 'Inciting Incidents' and each episode is just a series of inciting incidents, you know the kind of big stuff that happens in a movie that would change someone's life, you know force them to get out of the shit they're in, make them stop hurting that person they love, or just like cut their hair. But in the show they don't get out of it. None of them does that thing, they stay the same."

The cab driver pulled to the side of Fifth Avenue and took Thing 2's money. Thing 2 let it go like he had let go of the thought of ever having a birthday again. "Good luck with your dreams," said the driver.

To make God
appear
tell her a joke

a bad one

if she laughs
she loves you
as much as you've always
been promised

if not

There was one other person who entered the elevator with Thing 2, and that person stood against the back wall. Thing 2's cloud of frustration was mounting and filling the space. He stood ready to pounce out the door when they reached Thing 1's floor. He didn't know what he was going to say, but he imagined her opening her door, the look of betrayal, of disappointment. Or he feared she wouldn't be home, that he wouldn't find her again on any remaining Tuesday.

He put himself in her shoes, or tried. Pictured himself, standing apologetic in front of her, like staring at a reflection, standing at her door. He held the punching and screaming in, out of respect for the elevator passenger behind him.

The elevator doors opened onto the third floor. Standing in the hall staring at Thing 2 was another version of himself, locking eyes, his stunt double. They squared off. The double glanced at the other person in the elevator, who looked annoyed by Thing 2's refusal to step out. The other person in the elevator could only see an empty hallway, and pressed the door close button. Thing 2 jumped forward at the final second before the elevator shut, tackled his double.

They wrestled each other on the carpet, clawing at arms and faces and eyes. The stunt double lifted a wounded Thing 2 up against the wall and pulled his fist back to deliver a knockout. Thing 2 let the hallucination go, was alone again, and he dusted off and walked the seeming mile down the hall to Thing 1's corner door.

To become
God
at last

keep your plans
to yourself

No knock seemed good enough as Thing 2 stood at the door, closed hand half raised, but after a minute he found courage and managed a short tap-tap. He heard movement inside Thing 1's room. The edges of his flat mouth rose at the thought of reuniting.

A figure opened the door and stood in the doorway—tall, much taller than Thing 1—and made even more imposing by a towering red-and-white striped hat. Thing 2 stepped back. It was the Divine Bill, before his very eyes, at home in the headwear like this was normal, expected.

"Oh," Bill said, sour, "it's you."

Thing 2 was silent, the dictionary example of the word dumbfounded.

"She's not ready to forgive you yet. Come back tomorrow night."

Somebody standing behind the door slammed it in Thing 2's face.

Nearly everyone's life is a shaggy dog joke. Precious few are blessed with punchlines.

PART 4
Dual Projection

Someone walked up behind Thing 1 and covered her eyes with large inescapable hands. She was overlooking the river until seconds before, but then the hands blocked her view. She felt their size and angle and knew they weren't Thing 2's. A larger man, older, she thought, her nose reaching for his scent. She recalled the unmistakable way her father smelled, thought of his imposing size, thought of him standing behind her, always. But this wasn't him, of course, and the voice confirmed it.

"Guess who?" the voice said, familiar and generous, removing the inherent terror of forced blindness.

She grasped up for the hands and unblocked her eyes, whirled around and met the expectant face of the Divine Bill.

"No one will ever believe you," he said, like a script.

In the lull after his definitive statement, it was Bill's turn to register surprise. Thing 1 knew he was used to more shocked reactions and less "of course." He vocalized it.

"I know you," he said. "You're the one who's too good for my class."

"I'm having some issues," Thing 1 replied, an excuse.

"You and me both."

Bill suggested they get a bite, and they found a bistro on Tenth Avenue with an inconspicuous back courtyard.

It was a relief to be in his presence outside the loop of class. Thing 1 had believed, deep down, that Bill's daily vanishings in the park weren't the last she'd see of him. But she knew she'd never find the Divine Bill until she was truly as alone as the weatherman in the groundhog movie. Until she was the only person in the world on that second or fiftieth same day. But I didn't find him, she smiled to herself. He found me.

They ate in silence. It was enough for Thing 1 to be in Bill's proximity, and he sensed this enough to respect her reverence and shut up. She weighed the possibility of coming clean with him, revealing her repetition sickness. Maybe she'd recite the remainder of class, after she'd left, proving her omniscience just like he does in the movie, when he sits in a diner and recounts every detail of what happens seconds before it happens, like a god. What good would that do? He'd think she'd been listening at the door, or heard it from a friend. There was no convincing these Wednesday people. Bill might have been an icon, but like everyone else other than the Things, he was the opposite of immortal.

As Bill laid out crisp bills to overpay the check, he struck up.

"So. You're in school."

"Uh-huh."

"That means your friends have parties?"

"Yeah. There's always a party."

She was telling the truth. There was always a party. They went to one.

Thing 1 chose the party because she knew there was no chance that Thing 2 would be there. She wasn't prepared to reunite. Thing 2 had recently insulted the host's choice of outfit, and she had overheard. He wasn't invited.

The party apartment was small, but it was nestled on the top floor of a walkup on Bleecker Street and had roof access. Classmates often congregated there. Thing 1 opted for the apartment door rather than the roof ladder, even when there were voices coming from above. The room was full and barely acknowledged her when she stepped inside, another in a throng of familiar classmates. But then Bill followed. Everyone in the room stopped. Everyone in the room took a sip at the same time.

As the drunken randoms mobbed Bill by the door, he welcomed their hellos and hugs and life stories. Thing 1 grabbed a sparkling water from the fridge and found a spot on the couch. She watched Bill hold court and considered everyone around her, their Tuesdays up until this point, how few of them experienced the Divine via class or coincidence. She thought of their sad world without Bill, and how it had all just changed, thanks to her grace.

Bill and Thing 1 ended up sitting in chairs in the relative calm of the rooftop, watching the skyline until the other partygoers said their fan-soaked goodbyes and stepped down the ladder. "Yeah, man," they overheard some dude say as he descended, "it'll be sad when that guy dies."

"What is it about you?" Bill asked. "You seem different from all of them."

"I am different from all of them," Thing 1 said.

"I mean you don't act the same way around me."

Thing 1 thought for a beat. "I'm a little sick of your celebrity."

"You've only known me a couple hours."

"Sure, believe what you want to believe."

When they got back downstairs the host was passed out on her couch, sitting up with her head tilted forward. Bill went into the kitchen to do all the dishes. Thing 1 sat on the couch next to the unconscious host and watched Bill work. He was thorough, no hint of rush. She inhaled and exhaled.

In the corner was a tall red-and-white-striped hat, a novelty that she was sure no one wore in earnest. She couldn't take her eyes off it. After Bill finished he walked up to her, gave her shoulders a small squeeze with damp hands, and opened the door to go.

"Hey," she called out, and unlike with New Rochelle, it worked, and Bill returned.

"Hey," he replied.

"I need you to help me out."

Bill clutched the striped hat as they walked side-by-side, like peers, Thing 1 skipping to keep up with Bill's determined stride. He seemed to have all and none of the time in the world, a kinship. They spotted a guy alone in front of a stoop, facing away. They looked at each other.

"Your turn," Bill prompted, and Thing 1 obeyed.

She stepped up behind the guy and put her hands over his eyes, her little hands, a fake-out.

"Guess who?" Bill whispered in the guy's ear.

They teamworked this a few more times as they neared Fifth Avenue. Making people's nights was easy work for the Divine, its own reward. They walked past a bleary security guard and took the stairs up to Thing 1's room.

She was confident that Thing 2 would be at the door soon. Inside, she hatted Bill and told him the plan, gave him the script. When the knock came, Bill nailed it, like a true professional. She couldn't see Thing 2's dumbfounded face, but she trusted as she slammed the door.

Bill gave her the thumbs up.

"You look terrible," she said, reaching up to pull the hat from his head.

She woke up alone but didn't feel alone. Thing 1 carried the spirit of the Divine. It ignited her usual grogginess, a power.

She found her notebook and dusted it off. She'd gotten back to handwriting on recent Tuesdays, forgoing the word processor for ink, which somehow had the right kind of impermanence, on par with her own. She opened to a certain page, a quote she'd scrawled during a guest lecture in her sophomore year: *The problem with the Greeks is they haven't gotten over the death of Homer.*

She wrote out her entire encounter with Bill. With each jot she could feel the story slipping away. She would have to show Thing 2, at least, so he could share in it. Two memories were better than one, a safeguard against the forgetting. She put the notebook back where it had been, its vanishing place. Each morning the surface notebook was the same, but the words inside went somewhere irretrievable, a small magic.

The faces of Thing 2 came to her mind: she saw him right before the jump, saw him right after she had shoved the cinderblock backpack into his chest. In the hours leading up to his knock, every minute was loaded. She booted up her computer and made her away message *If Wednesdays were horses* and then took a hammer from her drawer and destroyed the keyboard.

An hour-and-a-half before the morning deadline, the 6:00 a.m. that hurled them back a day, Thing 2 knocked. Thing 1 answered. "I'm sorry," Thing 2 said. His smirk was unexpected, but Thing 1 grabbed control of the moment.

"Okay. Good. Here's how it's going to work," she said. "There's lots I want to say, and I'm sure there's lots you do too. It could take a million Tuesdays to do it. So what's going to happen is you knock, and I'll let you in, and I'll talk first, and then you can talk, and if I'm sick of the conversation I point to the door and you go out and knock again and we start over, somewhere different. You don't make demands and I decide when it's over, alright?"

"Alright," Thing 2 agreed.

He was in a euphoric state, ready to do whatever. She shut the door on him. He knocked. He attempted a hug. She shrugged it off and shut him out again. He knocked. She opened the door and he came in and sat on the bed. She sat down next to him.

"Did you accept the Lord at the last minute?" she asked.

"Fuck the Lord."

"Good. You're a groundhog worshipper now."

She pointed to the door.

He knocked and she let him in. He sat on the bed.

"Did you believe you'd lost me?" Thing 1 asked.

"For a little, yeah. I thought you didn't remember today."

"I remember today. All the todays."

"Why did you do that?"

"I was stalling until I could come up with a real punishment."

"I thought you'd gotten out."

"I don't want out."

She pointed to the door. Thing 2 left. This was a good form for day-repeaters, a shortcut, but not the fatal one. That shortcut was off the table.

Thing 2 knocked and she answered and they went to the bed together.

"You think I'm not suicidal?" she asked.

"No." Thing 2 looked down at his shoes.

"I'm just not today."

"I am. Or ... I was," he considered for a spell.

Thing 1's feigned abandonment had shaken Thing 2 out of his self-destruction. They looked at separate walls.

He looked back at her. Without looking at him, she pointed to the door.

"Our bodies don't age or change, you know. But our brains retain memories," Thing 1 said, standing, once Thing 2 had stepped back inside and sat down. "And the brain tells the body everything, so we're still dealing with all the consequences."

"Really?"

"You don't get it, cause you're a white dude."

"Okay."

"It's still trauma."

Even if Thing 2 spent a lifetime of Tuesdays as a girl, Thing 1 thought, he'd be a young, ageless one. It wouldn't be the same. She said what she had been waiting to say. "I don't want to hear how it felt, I don't want to hear what it was like. Not ever."

She pointed to the door. He went out. He knocked. Thing 1 opened up but didn't invite him to enter. She was at a loss for the next talking point. Thing 2 waited, obedient.

"Okay, you can ask me one question," she said.

"How did Bill get here?"

She ushered him to the bed and got her notebook out, opened it up and let him read the whole account. She was surprised by how self-conscious she felt as he finished, as if she were waiting for approval, for belief.

He closed the notebook and handed it back.

"You're amazing," he said.

She put the notebook away and pointed to the door.

He knocked and she answered.

"You can never do that to me again. Seriously," she stated.

"We're pretty close to never," he replied.

"I mean real never."

She waited in the doorway.

"I promise," he promised.

She shut him out, but opened the door before he could knock. He stepped inside and tried a hug and this time she allowed it. Forgiveness can take a lifetime to reach, and although the Things had an eternity, it only took them an hour to get there, knocking and answering.

He went to the bed and she locked the door, a symbol of finality. He scooted back, flattened his spine to the wall. She sat down in the desk chair across the way.

"You can ask me the other question now," Thing 1 said.

"You know it already."

"Ask it anyway."

"What happened, you know, after I died?"

"I'm not going to tell you that," she said, definitive.

He smiled, kicked his shoes off and pulled his knees up to his chin.

"I didn't think you would."

"You can ask me again in a hundred years."

Thing 1 felt exhausted. Thing 2 had inexplicable energy.

"How was your day?" he asked.

"I don't know, how was yours?" she replied, and Thing 2's smirk returned.

There was a knock on the door.

Thing 1 lost her lethargy, stood up and stepped forward, cautious. She looked back at Thing 2, who shrugged and stood beside her as she swung the door open to reveal a dream and a nightmare at once.

It was May. She wore a sloppy shirt and jeans, and she was unmistakable. May was a rock star, to them. Thing 1 had listened to her new album twice that day. She had never seen May in person, and in person her brown bangs were idols in their own right, her eyes a whole different story. Feline. A crush manifested. Thing 1 had to hold herself up on the doorframe to keep from falling.

"Good, y'all are together," May cooed. "Which one is better at memorizing?"

Thing 1 couldn't move. Thing 2 pointed at himself. May stepped forward and whispered in Thing 2's ear. She stepped back and gave the Things a once-over.

"I played a show at that address tonight, y'all should come." She winked at Thing 2 and squeezed Thing 1's quivering hand. "See you tomorrow, or you know, today, again."

May about-faced and the Things watched her walk halfway down the hall before Tuesday began abruptly again.

May and the Skipping Records

There once was a little kid in America and her name was May. She was different from all the other kids. The other kids skipped rope, or skipped breakfast. May skipped records. She couldn't help it. Every time she got close to the record player it started to skip.

"You can't go in the living room," the parents told her. "You can't come to our parties," the other kids told her. "You'll ruin our music." She had to sneak down by herself in the middle of the night and put records on. She could place the needle at any point, and the skipping would begin.

This was music, to her ears. For her, all songs were made of one line, repeated over and over. One night she flipped a switch and found slow motion. If the one line was slowed down, the songs seemed long, and beautiful. She listened in a new way.

In listening, she started writing. She started making slow records that were designed to skip. She started playing shows. People would come from all over to see her. May's skipping became music to their ears too. May got a house of her own and she filled it with record players.

One day she met two characters from another children's book. They were different colors but they looked alike; they even thought alike and spoke alike. They came to her show and said, "Hello, May. We love your music. We know you skip records. We skip days. Or, every day we skip back to this day, today. We are always skipping all the other days, the days that haven't happened yet. We're skipping them all."

May smiled and asked them if they wanted to join her band.

Thing 2 stood outside Thing 1's room at the tail end of the previous Tuesday. The door had just slammed, and the vision of the Divine Bill lingered, his words echoed. "She's not ready to forgive you yet. Come back tomorrow night." Thing 2 didn't move for minutes, stayed frozen until the reset grabbed him.

He was back in bed, his eyes bursting open to the sound of his roommate's alarm. He silenced the alarm and went back to sleep, dreaming of Bill and the impossibility of his presence. Hours of rest later, he rose and did what he'd never done voluntarily. Laundry. If life was going to be different from now on, despite the same day, Thing 2 wanted fresh clothes.

Once he was outfitted for a change he found the street below and went north, galvanized by all the questions Bill's presence had raised. He had so much time before he could return to Thing 1, and the progression of gum-littered sidewalk tiles he navigated seemed to light up with possibility. He had no idea what he was going to get into, and it was perfect.

On Fourteenth Street, at the southern edge of Union Square, the noise of New York reached a peak. His clothes already felt less pristine as they absorbed the erratic flow of aromas. He stood at the corner, basking in indecision, afraid of the WALK sign because that meant the DON'T WALK sign would soon start blinking.

Inches away from him, a car horn blared. Thing 2 smiled, callused against surprise and acclimated to the city's sharp edges. It had taken him years to ignore the honks. In the small city where he'd grown up, horns almost always indicated a friend in a car getting his attention for a wave or a ride.

This car honked again, insistent. Thing 2 looked down to make sure the curb was still under his feet. Then he did what he had worked hard to resist, he looked at the face of the honking driver. It was a face he thought he knew. The city stretched his skepticism. He'd had encounters with doppelgangers before, seeing someone who looked like an old friend and staring at them too long, thinking that maybe they were only staring back because he was also the doppelganger of someone they knew. He squinted at this glassed-in figure in the weathered gray sedan.

The driver rolled down his window and called out Thing 2's name. His real name. The driver's voice was confirmation. This was not just an acquaintance, but Shotgun. Shotgun was an old friend from home, and if Thing 2 had to pick, the first boy he had ever loved.

The light changed and Shotgun grew urgent.

"Get in."

Thing 2 jumped in the passenger seat like the sidewalk was lava.

Shotgun was named Shotgun because he was always calling it, but here on Tuesday, Thing 2 rode in the passenger seat. Shotgun came from a military family, but he had avoided enlisting via academic achievement. Thing 2 knew he'd ended up at the prestigious university south of the city, a state away. It wasn't unfathomable that he'd be driving across Manhattan on this day, but it was stirring. Thing 2 was silent as Shotgun tapped the steering wheel to the chug of a guitar and talked.

"It's wild, man. I was hoping I'd run into you, but. Big city, right?"

Thing 2 kept his eyes on Shotgun, who edged the car slowly through downtown traffic and laughed at the coincidence. This wasn't coincidence, Thing 2 thought. I've had so many chances to encounter you and so far I missed every one. Now their convergence seemed preordained. He was wearing clean clothes.

At last, Thing 2 managed a "What are you doing here?"

"There's a show tonight," Shotgun hooted. "Secret show!"

"Yeah?"

"You're coming. We're going!"

They ended up on the Manhattan Bridge at sunset, talking about warm past moments in the south. Their musical beacon that evening had also grown up in their hometown. Her name was May and she was phenomenal, proof that anomalies could grow from the uniform woodlands that surrounded their childhoods.

The exhilaration of crossing the East River hit Thing 2, another bending of the pact to stay bound to the island. This wasn't a struggle. He would have ridden anywhere with Shotgun, following the day into night. He had left the world, before, and he had left time itself. This was only Brooklyn.

Brooklyn wasn't terrible; it was even green. Shotgun parked along a park and they walked the few blocks to the venue. Shotgun paid the cover and they got their hands stamped side-by-side. The ink spelled *God is a concert.*

"I miss you, man." Shotgun grabbed hold of Thing 2's shoulder.

"Yeah, me too."

They made their way into the music hall. Shotgun drew Thing 2 along with him through the fattening crowd.

"Let's get to the front," Shotgun said and pulled Thing 2 by the crook of his arm. Thing 2 almost flinched, thinking of his wound from the previous day, and had to remind himself that he was unscathed and fully ready to be handled.

The noise of the crowd made it necessary to shout. They didn't. Thing 2 stood in the radiance of Shotgun's presence and stared forward at the crew setting up like they were a show in themselves. He tried not to look at Shotgun, out of fear that he'd disappear.

When the lights went down, he hazarded a glance. Shotgun was still there. Then May stepped out above them to a storm of applause. This was an exceptional appearance for someone as shut-in as May, a month that rarely arrives.

May played most of the show facing away from the audience, perched on a stool, mumbling the songs they all knew well as her band filled in the remaining sonics. The crowd lapped up the sludge of it, the promised idiosyncrasy. After almost a full set she dropped her microphone and turned, at last, pushed her bangs from her forehead and addressed the crowd.

There was news she needed to tell them, about the radio waves and the alien spacecraft. Shotgun was rapt. In this moment he and everyone else in the room believed the conspiracies she spun. Thing 2 saw her as a familiar, also trapped on her own wavelength.

She finished her rambles and grabbed her microphone back, signaling her band to begin the showstopper. The showstopper transported Thing 2 back to their hometown, to the same gray car that had spirited him from the street, to Shotgun blaring the album for the first time while they drove around seeing what friends of theirs were home. Shotgun was clearly transported too as May started lilting the first verse, and he placed an arm around Thing 2's shoulder.

Thing 2 followed suit, and then he turned and went further. This was a moment on another Tuesday, the Devil was a myth, and he kissed Shotgun's lips. He had to. Shotgun was the love of his life, or at least the love of his today, the today that had become his life.

Guitar swelled and Shotgun pulled away, mussing his own hair, an uncertain gesture. The look he gave Thing 2 was not at all a heartbreaker, but it made plain that he had to go. His mouth opened and he stepped back and was gone in the crowd.

Thing 2 turned his head back to see May, but she was no longer standing in the center of the stage, no longer singing. The band churned on, hitting each refrain harder. May was only a few feet away from him, crouched at the front of the stage, unraveling the microphone cord, obsessive and methodical, as if alone in an office cubicle, anywhere but a packed club, anyone but the center of attention.

She finished her task, freeing the microphone cord from any hang-ups, and she stepped off the stage, down into the audience. May held her arms out and spun, parted the crowd around her, making a wide circle. Thing 2 was corralled back closer to the door, but still in the first layer of the space that had been cleared for May.

May lay down on her back and brought the microphone to her lips and picked up the song where she'd left off, using her whole body to throw her voice to every inch of the venue. No one moved. On the final line May curled into a fetal ball and let the microphone go.

She crawled on all fours to Thing 2's feet, used his arms to pull herself up, clasped his hand and pulled him through the crowd toward the exit.

May led Thing 2 outside and across the street, into the dimly lit specter of the park. She didn't look back at him until they'd reached the bench where she wanted to stop. Then she dropped his hand and sat.

"Hey," May said, "I picked you out cuz I saw your man left." She produced a pack of cigarettes from her front pocket and offered him one.

"Hey thanks," he said and declined.

Thing 2 felt supernatural, the buzz of Shotgun's lips still staining his. He was emboldened to just be alongside an icon in the night.

"How often do you come to New York?" he asked.

"As often as I have to," May said, lighting and puffing. "What's your life like?"

If Thing 2 was going to tell anyone about Groundhog Day Day, about all the endlessness, it was May. He unfolded his stuckness, and May listened. And May believed.

"That's a tough one," she said when he was done telling. "Your favorite album of all time probably hasn't even come out yet."

"I know, and I didn't even know about your show, why don't I go see more shows, I could go to every show."

"Nah, just come to mine." She winked. "Maybe I'll remember you next time."

May dropped her cigarette and ground it into the dirt with her shoe.

"I like parks at night the best. I especially like that." She gestured with her finger above and behind Thing 2.

Thing 2 turned and saw it rising before him, floodlit, huge as the shadow of a Groundhog God. The answer. May said, "What?" and Thing 2 enlisted her help.

Thing 1 woke up the morning after May's appearance to the sound of New Rochelle leaving and did her usual dead-bolting. She logged onto her computer, using her spotless, undestroyed keyboard to message Thing 2: *what's the venue.* She called him on both phones and when they were done ringing she left the same message.

Then she got back in bed to wait. This time, she slept instead of staring upward at the wavering ceiling, and this time, she dreamt of May. Thing 1 found herself somewhere indoors, but rain was falling, and May came to her with unbuttoned jeans and incanted, "I'm from the future, or I'll put it simpler: I'm from tomorrow."

She woke up and retrieved a notebook and wrote a children's story. It came to her as sudden as May had, novel and witchy. She hadn't been happy with her writing until the day never stopped repeating, but what she churned out now in her notebook she placed with delicate reverence back on the shelf, sending it off into an uncertain, blind future.

By the time she picked up the phone to bother Thing 2 again he was already knocking on her door. She let him in.

"Did you see her too, or did I dream that?" he blurted, seeming equally baffled.

"It's real," she assured him. "May was right here."

Deception fit them both like a glove, and it was Thing 2's turn to wear it.

When Thing 2 said Brooklyn, Thing 1 didn't flinch. She would have walked barefoot from the city to upstate to see May perform. She wanted to be as early as possible. They ate preparatory noodles and went to the subway. On the steps down to the Brooklyn-bound platform they passed two men in full fatigues, carrying assault rifles. Thing 1 flinched, stopped and watched them ascend into the fading daylight before she continued.

The National Guard presence had thinned in the years since the long bad day, but these encounters always pushed her a little down inside herself. She made a note to avoid this station on ensuing Tuesdays. The voice of the station attendant came over the intercom, "There is an N as in Nazi train approaching Canal Street."

As the train barreled across the bridge Thing 1 looked around, electrified by May's words, unsure who among them was also trapped in the loop, lying in wait to reveal themselves. She listed off songs to Thing 2, songs she hoped May would play.

The robotic voice warned passengers to stand clear of the closing doors. Thing 1 wondered what it would be like if the movie they were locked in had a voiceover. She wondered what it would warn them away from.

"Let's get to the front," Thing 1 said, once they got stamped and entered the sparse crowd of earlies. Then she said, "What?" when Thing 2 smiled.

They glazed over through the opening act. Thing 1 had a singularity of focus. For the first time since the days had started repeating, she was exactly in the right place at the right time. May hit the stage. Thing 1 grabbed onto Thing 2.

May was an entirely different sort of star compared to Bill. Bill was detached from his brightness and carried it around at arm's length, confident. May's brightness seemed like it was burning her up from the inside. Thing 1 understood.

Thing 2 looked around for Shotgun, who should have been standing not far from where they were standing, but he was nowhere. He flashed back to the serendipitous intersection and thought of how many paths each day could take, how Shotgun could be trapped in traffic somewhere, lying dead somewhere without him. Even while May went to work mesmerizing the crowd, Thing 2 vowed never again to do the same night twice.

He let Thing 1 stand at the innermost layer of the circle that May had created in her final showstopper. On the previous night, Thing 2 had found himself tidal-waved by the unexpected, but tonight, everything flowed as he'd predicted. In her closing moment, May crawled to them and grabbed Thing 1's hand instead, spirited her outside to find the answer.

They reached the bench in the park and Thing 1 took a seat next to May. Her head spun.

"Hey," May said, "I picked you out cuz I can see your heart." She produced the pack of cigarettes from her front pocket and offered one. Thing 1 gave a faint nod. May placed both in her mouth to light them.

After a cautious puff, Thing 1 chanced, "It's happening to you, too? You're stuck in today, repeating it over and over."

"Like the movie? Nah. But also, yeah that sounds about right."

"You came to my room. Late last night, I mean, late tonight."

"Listen, I was in Baltimore late last night, but I'm not saying you're lying."

"I'm not. You were there."

"Hmm. I'm sorry that I don't remember, then." May winked.

Thing 1 sat and watched May smoke and let her own cigarette burn down to her knuckles.

"That guy you were with your man?"

"No. He's my ... familiar."

"I like that," May said and stood, taking the dwindling cigarette out of Thing 1's fingers and dropping it to the ground along with her own.

Thing 1 looked up and past May's shoulder and saw the answer, floodlit and monolithic and rising like a moon. A rock, the exact rock from the Things' shared dream. May noticed and turned to check it out too. She smiled and turned back to Thing 1.

"I bet you're a Taurus."

"I am, yeah," said Thing 1.

"I'm supposed to marry a Taurus," May said, and walked away into the darkness.

Thing 1 was still sitting and staring when Thing 2 appeared on the path. He stepped up so that he was framed by the rock, waved his hand with a flourish like a game show assistant, and bowed. She thought to applaud, but didn't.

"This was all you," Thing 1 said.

"Ta-da!" Thing 2 sang. "It's it, right? This is the rock. We had the wrong one."

"We had the wrong everything."

Thing 1 sprang up and ran to the base of the rock, clenching a crag in her fist, heaving herself up and scrambling to the top. She could see the film unfolding in front of her clearly here, a storyboard. They had to let Manhattan go, to find the right location. She turned and dangled her legs over the edge, waved for Thing 2 to join her.

"It's perfect," she said when Thing 2 reached the top and shuffled to her side.

"I'm sorry I didn't just lay it all out for you," he said. "I'm not really that into writing."

"No. This was better."

"I wanted to make it up to you."

"May brought you here last night."

"Yeah."

"What did she say?"

"That's between us. What did she say to you?"

"That's between us."

They decided to wait until morning on top of the rock, to claim it as their domain. Thing 2 recounted his night with Shotgun, and Thing 1 was thrilled by the possibilities.

"He's in town. Every Tuesday. Always," she urged.

"Yeah, but I don't know. We had our moment," Thing 2 said.

He knew that he and Shotgun would keep it best as longing. The show would never go well again, he was certain. All he'd want to do would be to hop in Shotgun's car and say, "We've been there already, let's go somewhere else."

Thing 1 was impressed with herself, and with Thing 2. For once they knew exactly what they were doing tomorrow, the one last mission they needed to complete together.

Thing 2 looked out across the trees to a pond, dark and bereft of birds.

"Wouldn't it be terrible to be an ugly swan? Because you couldn't turn into anything ... or just an ugly duckling that was really a duckling ... as opposed to a swan-ling?"

"The only reason he was ugly was because he was different."

"I know ... what a terrible world."

Five minutes later the sun rose and they fell.

It took Thing 1 and Thing 2 three repetitions to steal an allotment of film equipment from the Waterboys. First pleading, then attempting a break-in, then lifting the Waterboys' keys while they watched the groundhog movie. It took them two more days of successful thefts to realize how cumbersome the equipment was to haul on the subway and opt for a cab ride with Thing 2's cash instead. Before they rolled, they realized no superpower in the cursed world could develop the film from the shoot in time. They'd have to give up on film altogether and go video. They left the allotment sitting by the rock for others to see or steal.

It took three more repetitions for the Things to hit the sweet moment on the tenth floor of school when the new video cameras, stored in a room by the digital editing suites, were unattended and up for grabs. Thing 2 distracted the desk person, faking that he was locked out of his suite down the hall, and when the desk person followed him, Thing 1 skipped in and shouldered a hefty blue camera bag. She waited for Thing 2 to join her in the lobby and they walked out into a mess of students on Broadway. Wednesday people all.

"These kids walking around like they're invincible, when they're not. And we are, and we don't walk around like … that."

"Yeah, but they're feeling invincible because they're sure tomorrow's going to come. And we know it won't."

Thing 1 and Thing 2 tried to breathe deeply, surrounded by Wednesday people. Wednesday people with the void coming at them like a slow-moving cloud.

They had many preparatory days in them. Those days flew by like the cabs and trains they took over the bridge to Brooklyn, but they knew once they got to the shoot part they'd have to nail it. They wanted to complete the piece once. It had to meet their standards. Dressed in identical outfits and clutching New Rochelle's bow and the precious blue bag, they hurried to the rock below the ideal sky.

This park was better than Central because you could truly get lost. There were no towering buildings marking the edges to orient yourself. You'd have to walk toward the sound of music or the crack of bats. On a different Tuesday they might let the expanse consume them, but the rock was a magnet drawing them closer.

They knew the shots by heart. One of them would scale the rock first, with the bow, and the other would climb and shoot, and then they'd switch places. It didn't matter who was who, here behind and in front of the camera they were interchangeable figures. That was the whole point. When they pressed the record button, oxygen re-entered their world.

Somewhere in the distant green an impossible animal emerged from the ground.

The desk person was different when they returned to the tenth floor of the film school at sunset and signed into an editing suite. The clock was rarely ticking in their new existence, but tonight it was. The Things worked simultaneously at their stations. It was a two-sided piece, a dual projection.

This wasn't about plot.

It took hours but was effortless, the actualization of a vision. They exported the pieces to both tape and disc, bundled them up, and checked out of their suite. Sitting down at an old film editing deck in the hallway, they started on the hardest part, the letter.

Thing 1's theory was that every day they spent, every Tuesday repeated, was the beginning of an alternate timeline. In all these timelines, all these April 28ths and onward, the Things had disappeared from the face of the Earth, not to be found in New York City or anywhere else. Some people had to die for their work to be recognized. The Things just had to stay where they were in time, on Tuesday.

The editing deck they used as a desk had seen decades of use by the aspiring, each working long hours to hand-splice sixteen millimeter filmstrips together. Students had left their blood on this machine, an indelible sign that they were there. Inches from the splicing arm that had caused many little injuries, Thing 1 handwrote the title of their film and instructions for its screening, and then signed off with this, the final words of the vanished:

We are Sam Gainer and Anna Agarwal. Until Tuesday, April 27th we were film students in Manhattan. But now everyone believes we disappeared. We didn't. Don't look for us. We're here, in your hands.

They had a destination in mind for their piece, now bundled with the letter and ready: a gallery in Chelsea where they'd hoped to exhibit their work one day. The phrase *one day* had new meaning for them now.

On the walk northwest they took the chunk of cinderblock from Thing 1's dorm room.

"Why do you even have a chunk of cinderblock, though?"

"I forget, but I've had it since freshman year."

Tonight the cinderblock was for breaking into the art world.

They arrived at the broad window of the gallery. Inside they could see blank television screens. In their heads they projected their own work onto them. The block was deserted, all the exhibitions closed, no openings. Thing 1 checked for a security camera and found one, lensing them. She handed Thing 2 the chunk of cinderblock and he hurled it.

The window cracked but didn't break. He tried again and this time the shatter got catastrophic and the window came down. The alarm must have been silent. Thing 1 leaned through the opening and slid their bundle across the floor. The bundle came to rest at the center of the gallery.

They walked away toward the river and turned a corner. It would be gauche to wait around for the cops to roll up, the accolades to roll in. They were as established as they would ever be. No future needed.

Thing 1 and Thing 2 stood above the Hudson River.

"Is this where Bill found you?" Thing 2 asked. Thing 1 shook her head and gestured down the riverside with a wave. They were more relaxed at that last span of minutes before sunrise than they'd been in all the Tuesdays, and this surprised them. Now that they'd achieved artistic immortality, their actual immortality seemed less pressing.

Thing 2 sat on the ledge, aping the position he'd had on the roof of the film building, and Thing 1 joined him, forgiveness still coursing through her. She was jealous. He'd touched the divider between here and the other side, if not the other side itself.

Thing 1 knew Thing 2 knew what she was thinking about, that he was acutely aware of what this seating arrangement conjured. He knew better than to ask any questions, not yet.

"I'm so sorry, really. I know it sucked," Thing 2 said.

"I wouldn't do it like that." Thing 1 looked across to New Jersey as she talked, soft. "I wouldn't leave you alone. I'd just do it some way quiet a few minutes before 6:00 a.m. I'd just be gone from my body and you could drink a beer after, and then we'd be back to Tuesday again together."

"I'd miss your laugh, though, for that five minutes or whatever."

"Sometimes I miss you when you go to the bathroom."

Their romance was purely existential. In the end, if you can call a lack of any end an end, Thing 1 never once took her own life, and she never once died.

What doesn't kill you is something that happened to you.

PART 5
April 28th

In the sequel to the groundhog movie, the Things fall asleep by the Hudson River and wake up by the Hudson River. It is Wednesday. Their artistic achievement has snapped them out of the loop.

To make the groundhog proud, complete a project.

They embrace the brand-new day and each other, and head back to the Middle Village and the normalcy of the film school. They are reluctant at first to return, but find confidence in the freshness. Two days later the police show up to arrest them for their gallery break-in. Caught on tape, the police say. The gallery decides to show their work, inspired by the bold approach.

The Things go to prison. The movie becomes a different movie, a prison escape thriller. Thing 1 escapes and then helps Thing 2 escape and they jet off to a non-extradition tropical somewhere. Then in this faraway idyll they grow old together and die and get to see what comes after.

What comes after is they wake up in the ocean.

In the vicious sequel of real life, they woke up instead on Tuesday April 27th, as always. There was no way out of the loop. Thing 1 called Thing 2 to make a new pact, which she shared over coffee in the park under the monotonous blue daylight of their accomplishment.

"It's a sequel because there's two of us," Thing 1 repeated Thing 2's words, now with a different meaning. "And we did our best work separately."

Thing 2 agreed and they promised to spend every day apart, finding their own path. The only catch was that they had to meet up again in Thing 1's dorm room two hours before the reset, to share their experience. They needed the perpetual audience of each other to crowd-please.

"Who's going to forget an encounter with the missing Things, the vanished kids?" Thing 1 said, "Anyone we run into on whatever Tuesday will be the last people to see us alive. We are Bill. We create instant memories. No one will ever believe us."

On his first Tuesday with nowhere to be but in New York on a Tuesday, Thing 2 woke up and lay in bed and let his roommate's alarm beep on. He stretched and tilted his body into a backbend and craned his neck to look out the window behind him until he could see above the building across the street, upside-down.

It was his turn to cancel with the Waterboys. He typed up a new email: *I think we all need to see other people*, and clicked send.

Once his roommate woke and silenced the alarm, Thing 2 went out for a run, got three blocks away, limped back to his dorm room, and took a nap. He dreamt he was drafted. Shotgun was there in his dream house and they read the letter together and Shotgun eyed him with pride and lifted his hand up for a high five.

When you're dreaming, don't open your eyes to give someone a high five, because they won't be there.

Very awake, Thing 2 walked to the Eighth Street subway stop, boarded an uptown train to Times Square—a place he'd only go with visiting family—and headed to the Armed Forces recruitment station. The station was on a traffic island and topped by a bright digital screen showing all the magic of military service in high definition.

Brighter still were the neon T-shirts of the protestors standing in front of the station's doors, blocking Thing 2's way. He watched them instead of trying to push through. They were choreographed, a theater troupe in battle formation. An older man with long hair held a megaphone and repeated the lines of the recruitment video with a eulogistic sadness. "They simply volunteered," the crowd of performers chanted, echoing the older man.

The swarm of performers descended on Thing 2 and placed their hands on his chest, back and shoulders. They escorted him toward the station, but just before the doors, they dropped him back in a trust fall and lifted him up, holding him above their heads. He stretched out and let them hoist him upward.

There wasn't a plane in the sky.

On her first Tuesday with nowhere to be but in New York on a Tuesday, Thing 1 called her old boss from her old job, a gym near Madison Square Park where she had once worked the front desk, and asked to pick up a shift. There was a newer employee who had worked a double and could use the day off. Her boss told her to come on in. She took the same subway as Thing 2, but a few hours earlier.

Her old boss tossed her a logo'd T-shirt and she put it on and stood at the front desk from eleven to six, taking cards from members and swiping them through a slot to allow entry. She tried to make a connection with each one.

"Welcome," she said.

"Have a great workout," she said.

"I love you," she said.

Her boss asked her to do the boards. Doing the boards meant taking green chalk and writing up the class schedules for the next day on the black panels positioned around the fitness equipment on all three floors. Pilates, capoeira, etcetera.

Thing 1 freestyled and wrote words of warning in place of class names. *The groundhog is coming,* she chalked up. The boards would all be corrected by morning, by some confused fellow employee, but Thing 1 wouldn't know and didn't care.

The gym was dead at the end of Thing 1's shift. She stood at the front, her chin cupped in her palm and her elbow resting on the long desk. She enjoyed being bored. A slow-moving woman in her seventies stepped inside and ordered a smoothie at the bar adjacent to the desk. The woman walked to the desk while they prepared her drink, eyeing Thing 1 with recognition. They looked a little alike, generations apart but with similar faces under youthful oil and weathered wrinkles.

"Are you an artist?" the woman asked.

"Oh! Yes," Thing 1 responded, engaged again.

"See, I could tell, I can always tell. What kind of artist?"

"Well, um, I'm a filmmaker, but I also write, too."

"I see."

"Yeah, I'm in film school, right now."

"That's always been a kind of dream of mine, to make a film."

"Yeah."

"Maybe I could, someday, in my old age."

"I want to get sober," Thing 2 declared once they were met up, as promised, in the early morning hours, after their stories had been told. They could never wake up together, but they could sit up together in bed at the end of the day and eat their beloved dry cereal.

"Why," Thing 1 asked, "if you wake up fine every morning?"

"I think that's why."

"Okay. Maybe me too," she said.

Bars had been a large part of their city life before and after they turned twenty-one. Before and after the days stopped turning. Twenty-one was the age they'd have to remain. The lifestyle they could let go.

"What are you going to do tomorrow?" he asked.

"You mean today," she said.

"Today, yeah."

"You'll see."

Thing 1 looked across the room at her neglected computer. She no longer had the desire to create away messages, because every encounter on every Tuesday became an away message, left for each Wednesday person to recall, passed down from on high by nostalgia gods.

They worked on their last words because every new Tuesday was an ending.

"I've got a spaceship to catch," Thing 2 yelled at the security guard in his dorm lobby.

"When you see me again, I'll be gone," Thing 1 whispered to a hot cashew vendor on Fourteenth Street.

I wished for a city and it came true, Thing 2 wrote in blood from a pricked finger on the top of the Empire State Building.

Between the two of them, the Things attended every possible Tuesday class at the university, crashed other institutions as well, and concluded that working hard and getting good at one field was for losers.

They weren't accumulating knowledge—their young minds could only hold so much—and they weren't getting any older. They were simply sticking around longer, listening.

All that matters is how you interact with the people around you, the unselfish gifts you leave.

Thing 2 would only contact Thing 1 in the daytime if he needed a credit card. Thing 1 would only contact Thing 2 in the daytime if she needed a body to accompany her somewhere, to stand between her and the horrendous. He wasn't allowed to talk on these excursions, only block.

Freed from time and its trappings, she could cruise into and through any space without mortal peril, but the world of men was the world of men.

Thing 2 woke one day and found a handwritten note on his doorstep. It wasn't Thing 1's handwriting but it was Thing 1's voice. It told him to take a certain train to a certain stop, way uptown, and walk blocks into a stone-dotted wilderness. When he reached the spot the note designated, he felt drops.

It was raining.

He stood below the brief sun shower, a downpour he imagined he'd never again experience, and felt like his thunderstorm was outside instead of in.

One Tuesday the Things stayed indoors and called their mothers. They spent hours just listening to news from their hometowns, barely talking except to prompt their moms with more questions. They didn't mention upset, they didn't reveal their situation, but their mothers were worried upon hang up, concerned by this attention span, this anomalous loving correspondence.

One Tuesday a Thing returned to the film basement to see Bill and mouthed along with every word.

One Tuesday a Thing invited every student to the screening, hawking posters on the street and creating a mob.

One Tuesday a Thing rented every available copy of the groundhog movie in the Village and burned the tapes and discs on the sidewalk, and when Bill emerged he was enveloped in the smoke of his cinematic likeness.

A thousand Tuesdays later they decided they'd never watch the groundhog movie again, because it perverted their privilege as plight, gave them a sense that they should be striving to be better, a prescription for mindfulness, for a soul's progression, a self-better-ing, for an escape from the day, the opposite of what they wanted.

After ten thousand Tuesdays they hadn't seen the movie in so long they had forgotten the plot.

Was it about a groundhog or about a day?

If Thing 1 had been given a boy's name at birth, it would have been Thing 2's name.

If Thing 2 had been given a girl's name at birth, it would have been Thing 1's name.

But this didn't come up, not in all the endless days they spent apart, not in all the nights they ended together, recounting.

On a certain Tuesday, Thing 2 spoke to his roommate. It was the first April 27th he'd reached out, and he did it because he turned off his roommate's alarm, as usual, but then felt bad, as not usual. He grabbed onto his roommate's shoulder and shook him awake.

"Today is the last day of the best of your life," he said as his roommate rolled to consciousness. All his roommate said was, "Huh," but his roommate opened a cell phone and stepped outside. Thing 2 listened at the door, but could only hear that the conversation was tender.

Further downtown, the resident assistant on the other end of the phone hung up, happy, and left the coffee shop where she'd spent her early hours. She stole a cab from a frantic woman in a suit, and the woman slapped the window in anger. The cab went up Broadway instead of into SoHo.

Thing 2 dressed and sidled over to Sullivan Street and down. He arrived, unthinking, at an intersection he had been avoiding. A man with a gold watch strolled by. Thing 2, in a panic, asked for the time. The man told him. On any other day, it would have been crash time, but the cyclist went gliding past. The street remained glassless.

Thing 2 sat down on the curb and found he was laughing. The huge tongue of a dog collided with his face and licked and licked. Bear-like.

On a certain Tuesday, Thing 1 walked up the stairs in her building instead of down, and exited on the tenth floor. On the tenth floor she saw New Rochelle, and New Rochelle was entering another room. Whoever was inside had grabbed her collar and pulled. The door shut and Thing 1 walked to it, fist set to pound. She hesitated.

There was nothing to say. She went to the film building to meet with her mentor. Her mentor was a short gray-haired woman who'd worked in radio and lived across the street from the epicenter of the long bad day. She was fundamentally kind.

"I'm never going to be a real artist," said Thing 1.

"Oh please," tsked her mentor. "Have you made art?"

"Yes."

"Then you're an artist. All the rest is bullshit. History is unbelievable, so just live your life. Any experience you have is just adding to your life as an artist. You're there already."

The rest of that Tuesday belonged to bits and pieces of conversation. It belonged to every snippet blurted by a passerby that graced her all-too-alert ears. It belonged to the solid awareness she had of her own speech and its direct effect on those who heard it. And every step she took up Broadway—a diagonal arrow through the beating, slow-bleeding heart of Union Square—was a mark on the world.

Thing 1's theory about away messages was correct. Infinite futures were spinning from their everyday actions, their vanishing leaving a mark on every alternate Wednesday.

The Things assumed they were the only ones. But the Things were wrong there. They weren't the only ones.

Their experience wasn't unique. The ongoing sequel involves everybody. We're all immortal, as far as we will ever know, and at some point we don't get to find out what happens next.

I'll give you one, said the narrator, in voiceover. After all, you're not stuck in a movie. You're not characters in a children's book. You're a Wednesday person.

What happened next, on the Wednesday that followed their completion of the video and their breaking of the window in Chelsea, what happened next was someone found their work. When you vanish, your video art starts to look pretty good to a gallery.

The curators installed it within the month, while the disappearance was still hot, in their white high-ceilinged room near the West Side Highway. At the opening, the Italian introduced the piece. "They cut my class to make it," he joked to the gathered audience, before sombering over their absence.

The Things were there, though, waiting in the projector to captivate the walls.

Printed above the title of their piece, on a separate label, were the Things' real names and a description of their uncertain fate. An introduction to the mystery.

Then:

Thing 3 (b. 1983)
Nothing Hill, 2004
Two-channel video

On a summer day, months later, the Divine Bill stepped inside the gallery.

He nodded at a desk person who wasn't even looking up, and ascended some stairs to the second level, to the doorway of a small room, sectioned off from the big room by a curtain. He read the labels and scratched the stubble under his chin and walked through the curtain.

He squinted in the darkness of the minute between the video's ending and beginning, to see if anyone else was there with him, but he was alone in the world of the Things.

The video on the left wall starts out from Thing 1's point-of-view. A hand grips the rock and climbs, in shaky slow motion. The hand and the rock fill the frame. Careful grab by careful grab, the hand pulls its way to the top.

Thing 2 stands on the rock, five feet away, holding the empty bow. He draws the empty bow back, as if to fire a deadly arrow. Thing 1's point-of-view halts. Thing 2 lets go of the bowstring and Thing 1's point-of-view shudders as if struck, lurches back and falls, the rock rushes up into the sky and she lands on her back.

The point-of-view switches to Thing 2's. He leans over the edge of the rock and looks down at Thing 1, lying flat, in her identical outfit, wounded and still. A linger.

The video on the right wall starts out from Thing 2's point-of-view. A hand grips the rock and climbs, in shaky slow-motion. The hand and the rock fill the frame. Careful grab by careful grab, the hand pulls its way to the top.

Thing 1 stands on the rock, five feet away, holding the empty bow. She draws the empty bow back, as if to fire a deadly arrow. Thing 2's point-of-view halts. Thing 1 lets go of the bowstring and Thing 2's point-of-view shudders as if struck, lurches back and falls, the rock rushes up into the sky and he lands on his back.

The point of view switches to Thing 1's. She leans over the edge of the rock and looks down at Thing 2, lying flat, in his identical outfit, wounded and still. A linger.

In the dual projection, the core of the Things was transparent. They weren't different people, because on screen—the only place they existed from Wednesday on—they could be anyone, and what they were, then and forever, on a loop, was joined.

The Divine Bill looked back and forth between the climbing and falling Things, projected on the opposite walls. They were strangers to him. He hadn't met them in the past of this future.

But Bill found the familiar in their gaze, a pleasurable certainty the Things knew so well as they simultaneously looked upward, outward. He glanced into the alternating eyes of Thing 1 and Thing 2 and in them Bill came to understand what they already understood:

Tomorrow is the same, no matter how you slice it. It's not going to happen.

Back on Tuesday the 27th, in the cozy of the immortal dorm room, Thing 2 finished telling his story and Thing 1 finished telling hers. He was on the bed, his back to the wall, and she was in her father's chair. She didn't know it, but he had kept count.

"It's been one hundred years," he said.

"Hmm," she replied, and smiled.

"Can you tell me now, what happened after I died?"

The unaskable question, until.

"Sure," she said. "No problem."

He moved to the edge of the bed, ready to finally know the impact of his fatal jump from the roof. She leaned back and told.

"The truth is I have no idea how the world reacted. I was on the roof with my eyes closed and then I was in the stairwell down and I went out the emergency exit in the back of the building and came here. So, I can't tell you."

He nodded with an unexpected satisfaction.

"I sat where you're sitting and listened to our favorite song over and over until the day ended," she continued. "I wrote some poems, but they weren't for you, they were for the Wednesday people."

"Okay," he said.

"I write for the future."

"Do you remember any of them?"

"Maybe," she said. "Ask me again in another hundred years."

The bed beckoned her and she went and sat beside him.

"I kind of want us to use our real names from now on," she said. He leaned against her shoulder. They waited for the dawn to wash their bodies clean of the extra day.

Their anticipation cast a shadow that looked like one unbroken figure, like candles melted together, against the opposite wall. They stared at the shadow and the shadow stared back, as if across the desk at a job interview, the loaded question dangling.

Where do you see yourself five seconds from now?

Forever Thanks

to Emily Kiernan, for her belief in this book at the beginning of its journey, and to Peg Alford Pursell, for giving that journey a perfect destination

to Antonio Monda and Bill Murray, for the true story, the spark

to all my classmates at Tisch, for weathering the long bad day alongside me, and for inspiring every aspect of the Things

to my family, for sending me to New York and leaving me there

to Katherine Hurbis-Cherrier, Darrell Wilson, Barbara Malmet, Speed Levitch, Chan Marshall, Bill Viola, Eija-Liisa Ahtila, and Shirin Neshat, my guiding lights

to Malcolm, a boundless and generous talent

to Merkel, the other half of my shadow

Henry Hoke wrote *The Book of Endless Sleepovers* and the story collection *Genevieves*, which won the Subito prose prize. His work appears in *The Offing, Electric Literature, Hobart, Juked*, and the flash noir anthology *Tiny Crimes*. He co-created the performance series Enter>text in Los Angeles, and has taught creative writing at CalArts and the University of Virginia Young Writers Workshop. *Sticker*, a memoir, is forthcoming from Bloomsbury's Object Lessons.